MURDER AND THE SECRET CAVE

A High Desert Cozy Mystery - Book 2

BY

DIANNE HARMAN

Published by: Dianne Harman
www.dianneharman.com

Interior, cover design and website by
Vivek Rajan Vivek
www.vivekrajanvivek.com

ISBN: 978-1519432834

CONTENTS

ACKNOWLEDGMENTS

To all of you who take the time to read my books, thank you. Without loyal readers like you, I wouldn't be a writer, and it's something I've come to love! Each and every one of you is very important to me. I always appreciate your emails with their thoughtful comments, praise, and often suggestions for new books.

I want to thank my husband's uncle, Bill, who many years ago invited us to his compound outside of Palm Springs, California. There were several artists living in the four houses which surrounded a central courtyard. The memory of that place has stayed with me for over thirty years. I'm so happy I was able to recreate that magical place in my High Desert Cozy Mystery Series.

There are two people who make me and my books look good, my husband, Tom, and my friend Vivek Rajan. Tom patiently reads each book several times with a sharp eye for inconsistencies which I've missed. He's an idea man and many a twist and turn in a plot has come from his fertile mind. Vivek is responsible for the book covers and the formatting – things which totally escape my technologically challenged mind. He is also a genius at social media marketing. I've learned so much from him. Thanks to both of you!

And I would be remiss if I didn't thank Kelly, my boxer puppy, for forcing me to take an occasional break from writing to let her out and play with her. I would probably atrophy without her. Thanks, Kelly, and I'm so glad to be able to return our house to some sense of normalcy now that you're getting far better in your choices of what to chew on!

Amazing Ebooks & Paperbacks for FREE

Go to www.dianneharman.com/freepaperback.html and get your FREE copies of Dianne's books and Dianne's favorite recipes immediately by signing up for her newsletter.

Once you've signed up for her newsletter you're eligible to win autographed paperbacks. One lucky winner is picked every week. Hurry before the offer ends.

PROLOGUE

Randy Jones sat at the old scarred wooden table in his one room shack and looked at the papers the appraiser, Marty Morgan, had left with him stating her fee and the estimate for the length of time it would take her to prepare an appraisal report for his Native American artifacts collection. He sat drinking his usual bourbon and branch water out of a tin cup. Dressed in worn jeans and a worn blue denim shirt, he looked every bit like the desert rat people called him when referring to him. Long unkempt hair, a missing tooth, and a shaggy beard had led to that description.

The old shack looked as unkempt as its owner with its weather-beaten wood siding and a door that sagged and hung from a broken hinge. The inside was just as unappealing. A single unmade iron bed with sheets that looked like they hadn't been washed for a long time were covered with a dirty blanket. An old iron stove Randy used for cooking was in the corner of the room. A single lantern was on a table, providing light when the sun set. He felt the cool breeze on his back as it blew through the open door.

He could tell that the appraiser had been very impressed with the quality of his Native American artifacts, particularly the pieces he'd shown her in his secret cave. He knew that the word Indian wasn't politically correct nowadays, but privately he always thought of it as his Indian collection.

Randy told the woman he didn't want to waste her time and his money finding out about the authenticity or the history of the items. He knew full well all about the artifacts and knew they were for real. He'd said that whoever bought the collection would already know about them as well. The only thing he wanted to know was how much money he could get for the collection. He had a pretty good idea what it was worth, but with the shooting pains in his chest along with the constant hacking cough getting worse, sometimes his mind wasn't as sharp as it used to be. Having something in writing would give him some bargaining power with the buyer.

That was the last thought Randy Jones ever had as the tomahawk plunged into the back of his head, killing him instantly. The killer heard a car door slam and quietly slid out the door, leaving Randy Jones dead on the floor with the tomahawk buried in his head. The killer quickly disappeared among the nearby boulders and rocks that surrounded the shack.

CHAPTER ONE

Randy looked around the cave where he kept his best Indian artifacts – it had been his secret and his alone, but with the news the doctor had given him yesterday, he knew he'd have to share it with someone very soon. He'd found the secret cave years ago and was certain it had been home to Indians who'd lived in the area from the number of arrowheads and other artifacts he'd discovered in it. It was big enough he figured several families had probably occupied it. Over the years he'd brought in tables and a couple of lanterns that took away the eerie, mysterious nature of the cave. He'd gotten used to the cobwebs and figured if anyone ever did stumble into it, they'd be so scared they'd leave immediately. It was the one place that kind of spooked Randy. He knew old desert rats like himself weren't supposed to believe in spirits and things of that nature, but he was pretty sure there were some spirits in the cave leftover from the Indians.

He took the pack of unfiltered cigarettes out of his shirt pocket and shook one out, putting it between his lips in the indentation that thousands of others had made over the years. *Don't care what no doctor says, not givin' these up, even if they did cause the cancer the doc says I got.*

Before he could light his cigarette, Randy started coughing, doubling over in pain. He waited a few moments for the spasm to leave his body, lit the cigarette, and took a swig from the pint whiskey bottle on the table next to him. He took one of the pills the doctor had given him yesterday for pain and washed it down with the whiskey, waiting for it to begin to work its magic. While he waited for the pain to subside, he looked around the cave at his treasures. He kept the best of the best here, out of sight. The second rate stuff was in his shack and the shed behind it. Some people knew about the stuff he kept there, but the only one who had seen what was in the cave was Colin, and he'd only been in it once. He was pretty sure Mary had suspected Randy had a secret cache.

He thought about what Lucy, the photo department clerk at the drug store had told him about the appraiser, Marty Morgan. Lucy said she was good people, and since Marty was an appraiser and both of them had Lucy develop their photos, she thought Randy should meet her. Even though Lucy had been suggesting it for several months, he'd always found a reason not to. Now he had a very big reason to meet her – the Grim Reaper.

Never planned on doin' nothin' like this, but since it looks like I'm gonna bite the big one real soon, probably better get somethin' in writin', so I can show it to a couple of people who'll want to buy my stuff, not that the money's gonna do me much good now. Only relative I got is my boy, and I ain't seen him since he was two years old. I didn't want nothin' to do with him or my wife when they left, and I'd be willin' to bet he never wanted nothin' to do with me neither. Guess that's what happens when yer' a desert rat, least that's what my wife said when she took the kid and left for Los Angeles.

She tol' me I'd never make nothin' of myself , and she was leavin' fer good, and so she did. If she saw this stuff, she'd know jes' how wrong she was. Since I haven't seen my son in almost forty years, no reason for me to give him any money I get fer my collection. Don't know if I'm still married or not, but sure don't want her to get a cent. She's the one who left. Would kinda like my son to know jes' how successful his ol' desert rat dad was. Maybe I'll try and find him. Give him a call and tell him now I'm a millionaire, but he and his mother ain't getting' none of it. Serve 'em right, it would. Then again, when I'm dead maybe somebody'll call 'em and tell 'em I had a lot of money, but they ain't getting' none of it.

He crushed his cigarette out and put it in the empty can of pork and beans he used as an ashtray and at the same time expertly pulled another cigarette out of the pack and lit it. *I 'spose that's why they call these dang things "cancer sticks" cuz when you smoke 'em back-to-back like I do, ya' get cancer,* he thought as he took a deep drag off the newly lit cigarette.

I know it's one of the best collections of Indian things, probably in the world. That gold I found early on sure helped me be able to afford a lot of the black market stuff. Problem is, I can't sell it legitimately. Probably have to sell it all to Colin. He's been hot fer me to do it forever.

Think I'll live out my last days down in the Caribbean on one of them lil' tropical islands. Get me some rum and an island mama. I could do with that. Been a long dry spell fer me. Yeah, that's what I'm gonna do. Have that appraiser write up something 'bout what this stuff is worth, show it to Colin, that guy who's so hot to trot, and tell him what I want fer it. As anxious as he is to get his hands on my collection, it should be easy. Course there's also that hoity-toity doctor I keep runnin' into at the shows. He'd probably be interested. Maybe I can set up a little biddin' war between 'em.

He put his cigarette in the bean can, left the cave, and like he always did, rolled the rocks in front of the entrance to conceal it from view. Years ago he'd had a couple of large fake boulders made that he could easily roll in front of the entrance, so even if someone was trying to find the cave, which he didn't think anyone knew about, the rocks would look like all the others on the small rocky ridge. Nothing else indicated the treasures that lay hidden inside.

CHAPTER TWO

Marty Morgan rolled over and looked at the clock on her nightstand which read 6:15 a.m. She groaned and knew she was through sleeping for the night. Her inner clock was still on Chicago time. She looked down at her big black Labrador retriever, Duke, who was still asleep on his dog bed next to her.

She'd gotten in late last night after driving from the airport in Ontario, California, to the compound where she lived in High Desert with her sister Laura and two men who had become like family to her. When she opened the gate to the compound she saw Les, the artist her sister had been with for years, and John, the owner of The Red Pony food truck, sitting at the picnic table in the communal courtyard, having a late glass of wine. They told her Duke hadn't slept the entire five days she'd been gone, although both of them had tried to coax him into their homes which surrounded the courtyard. They said he'd laid next to the gate, looking under it and waiting for her return, his customary place whenever she left the compound. He became ecstatic when he finally saw her. She was amazed that a dog that big, all seventy pounds of him, could twist into curlicues whenever she returned to the compound.

When she moved to High Desert after her husband told her he was divorcing her and marrying his secretary, one of the first things she'd done was visit the animal shelter in Palm Springs and taken home a little black puppy. Although Duke was a constant source of joy to her, he did have one little issue that at times, drove her nuts. A few months ago he'd developed a new habit. He refused to step out of the compound. No amount of dog treats, bologna, bones, or hamburger meat could entice him to put his feet on the desert sand. There were times when she wanted to take him for a little walk outside the compound, so both of them could communicate with the beauty of the natural desert surroundings, but Duke would have none of it and steadfastly refused to leave the compound.

John had suggested dog booties. He told her he had a friend with the same problem, and once the dog had booties on her feet, she'd go anywhere. Resigned to looking ridiculous with a seventy pound dog wearing pink booties, the only color they came in according to the Internet site she'd bought them from, she put the booties on Duke. She opened the gate of the compound and for the first time in months, Duke willingly walked beside her. Of course her sister and the two men teased her unmercifully about Duke's pink booties. Many months ago she'd resigned herself to the fact that someday she would probably see a picture of Duke and her on the front page of the local paper, above the fold, Duke resplendent in his pink booties, which was quite a contrast to his black coat.

She thought back to the last few days which had been more than interesting. Dick Cosner, her sister Laura's boss at the insurance company, Alliance Property and Casualty Company, had asked her if she'd be willing to go to Chicago to do an appraisal for one of their wealthy clients. Although the client now lived primarily at his home in Palm Springs, he still maintained a condo in Chicago where he'd lived prior to moving to the desert. Even though he now worked from his desert home, his formal business headquarters was still in Chicago.

As she recalled, the conversation had gone something like this: "Marty, it's Dick. We have a very wealthy client who lives in Palm Springs most of the time, but he also owns a condominium in Chicago. He's an idiot savant and has one of the finest private Tiffany glass collections in the United States."

"Dick, I'm at a loss here. I have no idea what an idiot savant is."

"Well, usually it means a person who's highly knowledgeable about just one subject, but clueless about everything else. They almost need a keeper. In our client's case, he's knowledge about two subjects, wall street finance and Tiffany art glass, and he has a personal assistant who takes care of everything else for him."

Dick continued, "He's a hedge fund broker, a very successful one. He only has five clients, but he does so well with them he's made millions, could even be in the billions, but here's the interesting part. Somehow he became fascinated by Tiffany art glass and started collecting it years ago. He buys from auction houses throughout the world and even rents one floor in a warehouse building in downtown Chicago where he stores his collection of Tiffany art glass.

"Of course, the best of the collection is in his waterfront high-rise condo on Lake Michigan and at his home here in Palm Springs. You'll be appraising the items in his condo as well as the collection in the warehouse. His personal assistant will accompany you and do whatever you need him to do. He said he has the time right now because his boss is currently in Palm Springs. I told him you'd need two or three days to properly appraise the items, and he said that wouldn't be a problem. Hope you agree to take this one. As I said, it should be interesting."

"I just finished an appraisal yesterday, so you caught me at a good time. When would you want me to go?"

"I'd like to say today, but that's probably a little too short of notice. Why don't you drive to Ontario and fly out of there tomorrow? You can get into Chicago at a decent hour, get a good night's sleep, and be ready to go day after tomorrow. If that works for you, I'll make the flight and hotel arrangements and get back to you."

"Sounds great. Thanks, Dick."

"One other thing, Marty. From what his personal assistant told me, his house here in the desert is loaded as well. Looks like I'll need you to also do those items."

A few hours later Dick called back with the necessary travel information, and the next day she was off to Chicago, Duke's forlorn look notwithstanding. Both Les and John refused to walk Duke with his booties on, so Marty had enlisted her sister's help. Marty knew the only reason she'd agreed to walk Duke was because Marty had promised to go to a bookstore in Chicago that Laura said was well-known for having the best books on psychic phenomena. Laura was a modern day psychic who eschewed turbans and crystal balls for business casual clothing. No one who ever met Laura would suspect she'd been a participant in a paranormal study conducted by UCLA that found her to have a very high level of extra sensory perception. It wasn't something she talked much about, but from time to time, she was able to help people with her "inner knowing." The list of books she'd given Marty was huge. Marty managed to have most of them shipped by UPS to Laura rather than trying to bring them back with her.

She looked again at the clock and realized she must have dozed off, because it was now 7:00 a.m., an hour when Laura and John would be up and about, so taking Duke for a walk wouldn't wake them up. She knew Les often liked to work on his paintings until the early hours of the morning and then sleep in until late in the morning. Marty got out of bed, put her bathrobe on, and walked to the front door where Duke stood with his leash hanging from his mouth, patiently waiting for her to put on his pink booties.

CHAPTER THREE

"Hey, Lucy, what's up?" Randy said to the woman working in the photo development department of the Hi-Lo Drugstore in High Desert, the small town located thirty miles outside of Palm Springs, California.

"Just finishing up some photos I got from Marty Morgan, that appraiser I tol' ya' 'bout. Lawdy, if she don't see some of the bestest stuff. This latest one's got some fer real Tiffany lamps in it. She's so 'portant some rich guy in Chicago paid her to go there and take a look-see at his stuff. She uploaded her photos to me, and I jes' finished 'em. She's comin' in later today to pick 'em up. Man, never seen nothin' like what's in them photos other than in some fancy magazines. Must be fun, bein' an appraiser and seein' all the expensive stuff other people own. So what's up with ya', ol' blue eyes?"

Although most people referred to Randy as a desert rat, Lucy and some of the other people in town called him "ol' blue eyes" because of their color. She'd never seen another human being with eyes like his. They looked like a deep Alpine lake she'd seen in a magazine one day when she'd been browsing through it on her lunch hour. They were almost eerie, and it was hard to look directly into his eyes. They seemed to be bottomless.

"Funny you'd mention her. You've seen some of my Indian

things. Thinkin' maybe I need to get me some kinda appraisal on 'em 'afore somethin' happens to me."

"Randy, yer' too mean to have anything happen to ya'. Why'd ya' go and say sumpin' like that? Everybody in town knows a mean desert rat like you's gonna outlive us all. Only thing that might get ya' are those cancer sticks ya' can't stop smokin'. Saw somethin' on the tube the other night that those things are killers. Might wanna think 'bout quittin'," she said.

"Jes' may be doin' that, Lucy, jes may be. Now be a good girl and give me the telephone number for that appraiser yer' so high on."

"I'm a little long in the tooth to be called a girl, ya' ol' fool." She looked on her cell phone for her contacts list and gave him Marty's number. "When ya' talk to her, tell her I said that latest batch of photos she sent me is somethin' else."

"Will do. Think I'll go on home and give her a call."

"Does that mean I'll get to see all yer' purty things if she appraises them?"

"Probably does, knowin' how ya' can't keep from lookin' at 'em," Randy said and winked as he walked out to his truck.

As soon as Randy left, Lucy wondered if she should have told him someone had been asking about him, but since the man had paid her one hundred dollars, maybe it would be better if she didn't say anything. In a town as small as High Desert, there wasn't a visitor center or a place like that to get local information. Hi-Lo filled that need. The store carried about everything anyone living in a small town would ever need from cigarettes to cosmetics to necessities like bread and milk. Sooner or later almost all of the residents of High Desert passed through the doors and were greeted warmly by the staff, particularly by Lucy whose photo department was near the front of the store.

Lucy loved people and often told Jake, her husband, when they were at the Road Runner Bar on Saturday nights, that she had the best of all jobs. Thinking of the Road Runner Bar made her think of the man who had come in the day before and asked her questions about Randy. Randy was a regular at the Road Runner, and she didn't think she and Jake had ever been in there when Randy wasn't firmly planted on a bar stool, bourbon and branch water in hand.

Yesterday, a man she didn't recognize had walked up to her counter. She'd looked at the slender man in his mid-40's and knew he wasn't a local. He wore a lightweight blue sport coat over a white open-collared shirt and jeans that looked like they'd just come from the cleaners. Polished loafers encased feet that wore no socks. His hair had been professionally groomed, and from the well-maintained stubble on his chion, it was obvious he hadn't visited High Desert's barber to achieve the look.

"Excuse me, miss. I just spoke with the manager, and he told me you might be able to help me. He said you know everyone in town. I'm trying to locate a man named Randy Jones. I believe he lives around here. Do you know him?"

"Maybe I do, and maybe I don't," Lucy said. "Why do ya' wanna know?"

"I knew him a long time ago, and thought it would be kind of nice to renew our friendship."

Lucy took a long look at the man. She may have lived in a small town all of her life and failed English class twice, but street smart she was. Very street smart, and the vibes she got from this man told her he wasn't being honest with her. Why a man like the one in front of her would have anything to do with an old desert rat like Randy Jones was really strange. Something else bothered her about his appearance, but she couldn't put her finger on it.

The man took his wallet out and said, "I need a pack of Desert Springs cigarettes. Oh, by the way, look what I found. Well, I'll be darned. Don't that just beat all? I found a hundred dollar bill that has your name on it. Why don't you take it? Now where were we? Oh yes, I asked if you knew a man named Randy Jones." He put the hundred dollar bill on the counter in front of Lucy.

Lucy looked at the hundred dollar bill and looked up at the man, an inner struggle clearly taking place in her mind. She desperately needed the money. Clerks at the Hi-Lo weren't paid very much, and the toothache she'd had for months was bothering her more every day. She'd seen Dr. Morton when it had started, and he told her if she could pay him one hundred dollars or as he called it, "earnest money," he'd do the root canal, and she could work out a monthly payment for the balance. She touched the aching tooth with her tongue and came to a decision.

"Yeah, I know Randy," she said, pocketing the hundred dollar bill. "He lives in a shack a coupla' miles off the main road outta town. You'll see a sign for a roadrunner crossing. Take the first dirt road on the right past the sign to where it intersects another dirt road that comes out of a canyon. Take a left on the dirt road that runs into the canyon, and he's up 'bout a mile. Can't miss it cuz there's an ol' tumbledown shed behind his shack. The place is surrounded by lots of big boulders and rocks. You'll also see a whole bunch of rusted stuff he's got out in front of his shack. Never know when ya' might need sumpin. Can't miss it. Plus, he's also got a rusted ol' orange truck that's probably sum' kind of antique. Ya' can park where you see his truck and walk up the path to his place."

A customer walked over to the counter and Lucy said, "Been nice talkin' to ya'. Good luck and thanks. See ya' around."

"Thank you. If I need something more, I'll be back.," the man said, turning away from Lucy and the customer as he walked over to the front door and out to his black Cadillac Escalade. Lucy watched him as he got in the big SUV.

CHAPTER FOUR

Luke Peterson looked at all the old trucks and cars as he walked through the parking lot of the Hi-Lo Drug Store to where his shiny black Cadillac Escalade SUV was parked.

Well, with my SUV, they're never going to mistake me for a local, that's for sure, but I don't care. I've paid my dues. Anyway, Dr. Rosenbaum said he thought it was a good idea for me to buy the SUV. He says I've come a long way in therapy.

As he drove out of town he thought back to what had led him to come to High Desert, to finally find and confront his father. His mother never told him anything about his biological father, and when she'd died at an early age from breast cancer there was no way for him to find out anything about his father. The man his mother had been living with had never adopted him. When she died, he'd taken Luke to the county juvenile authorities and told them his mother had died, and he needed to become a ward of the court.

The next few years were a haze of going from one foster family to another. When he was twelve, usually a very hard age to find anyone who was willing to accept a male foster child, much less adopt one, he'd been adopted by the Peterson family who were trying to fill the hole in their hearts that the death of their son had left. They were good people and good to him. When they discovered he had an aptitude for computers, they sent him to a special school to take advantage of his skills.

At sixteen, he'd designed his first computer app, a game that had been bought by one of the foremost computer gaming companies. They'd been so impressed with Luke's abilities that the gaming company told the Petersons they wanted to hire Luke, even though he was under the legal age for full-time employment. The Petersons wanted Luke to go to college and were very resistant to the idea that he would quit school and not even graduate from high school. A compromise was finally reached, one where Luke would graduate from high school and then go to work for the gaming company for a ridiculously high salary for a young man barely eighteen.

He smiled thinking back to the years that followed with one game app after another being produced, all huge money makers for the company. His salary also increased to astronomical heights. Soon he bought the Petersons a new home and a new car for each of them. Although he was very close to them he still woke up in the middle of the night wondering about his father, the father who had never tried to get in touch with him.

Luke's fear of abandonment issues stayed with him in spite of how wealthy he became. His relationships with women never made it to the stage of marriage, even though he'd really cared for several of them. When push came to shove, he just couldn't fully trust anyone. He finally realized he needed some professional help and contacted Dr. Rosenbaum, a psychiatrist whose name he had heard of from several people in the industry.

After many therapy sessions and quite a bit of progress, the doctor suggested Luke hire a private investigator to see if he could find his father. Luke had been two years old when his mother had left his father and his memories of his father were nonexistent. He had no idea where they'd lived before coming to Los Angeles.

When his mother died, the man she'd been living with gave him a plastic bag with her wallet and a couple of other things in it and told Luke he didn't want any of the things in the bag. It was all he had of his mother's personal belongings, and no matter how many foster homes he'd been in, the plastic bag was always under his pillow. Even as a grown man, he slept with it under his pillow. Dr. Rosenbaum had tried to get him to change that particular behavior pattern without any luck. Over the years Luke had examined the contents of the bag time and time again, seeking some link to his first two years and his father. There was nothing.

One evening he was unwinding with a glass of wine looking out the window at the deep apricot color of the sky as it turned to blue over the Pacific Ocean. He knew buying an oceanfront condominium in Malibu, an exclusive seaside area of Los Angeles, had been a luxury, but as much money as he was making and as hard as he was working, he'd justified it. Luke had come from a meeting with his attorney and was still dressed in the sport coat and slacks he'd worn to the meeting. Even though he could wear whatever he wanted with the status he had as a "video game inventor," he wanted to show the world he'd made it by dressing like bankers or lawyers would dress for a meeting. He walked into his bedroom and saw a piece of plastic sticking out from under his pillow where his housekeeper had evidently not placed the pillow squarely on the ever present plastic bag like he'd instructed her to do.

Luke picked up the bag and walked over to the window seat that offered the same spectacular view he'd just seen, but the passing several minutes had changed the color of the sky and ocean so now they appeared to meet and were the soft blue of the early evening. He sat down and took out the contents of the bag. It had been several years since he'd looked at them, although he had them committed to memory. Simple things. A scarf, a wallet, and a locket. The sum total of his mother's life. How he wished she were alive and could see the success he'd made of his life.

He brought the scarf up to his nose and inhaled a vague perfume scent, amazed there was any scent left after all these years. He idly looked in the wallet and recognized the coins and other items. *Nothing new there,* he thought. He picked up the last item, the locket, and ran his thumb and index finger over it. It was sterling silver, the only thing of any value his mother had owned when she died. He remembered seeing it on her. As he thought back to the last time she'd worn it, just before she'd gone into the hospital and never returned, it popped open. He stared at it, incredulous, and shook his head. Luke couldn't believe that after all the years he'd tried to open it and couldn't, having finally decided that it wasn't the type of locket that could be opened, tonight it opened.

Luke eased his thumbnail between the two sides and gently pried it apart. There was a photograph of a man inside the locket. He was bearded, with a cigarette between his lips and had a baby sitting in his lap. Luke stared at it, unbelieving. *It must be my dad. That must be me.* His hand shook as he carefully ran his thumbnail around the old photograph, and it fell out. He turned it over and on the back was written "Randy and Luke Jones."

He looked away from it and tried to concentrate on the surf line as the incoming tide crept up the sand towards his condominium, while evening surfers tried to catch the last wave of the day. His heart was thudding, and his hands were clammy. He honestly didn't know what to do. Finally, after all these years, he had the name of the man who was his father. It wasn't much, but that photograph was his legacy, and he decided at that moment to follow it wherever it led him. Along with the shock of finding the photograph a sudden surge of anger overcame him, anger he had never felt before. Anger that was strong enough that it made him feel like killing the man in the photo – the man who had caused him so much pain during his entire life.

Luke pressed Dr. Rosenbaum's number into his phone, and it was answered within seconds. "Yes, Luke. What is it? I don't think you've ever called me in the evening like this. Is something wrong"

He told the doctor what had happened and asked the doctor what he thought he should do with the information.

"Luke, before I answer your question, tell me something. You sound very angry, are you?"

"Doctor, at this moment I feel I could kill my dad for what he's done to my life. Maybe it's normal, but I've never felt like this before."

"I think we should talk about it. Can you come in tomorrow? I have an appointment I can cancel. I think it's more important for you and me to talk about this anger. Can you come in at 3:00?"

"Yes. I'll be there. Now what do you think I should do with this information?"

"Call the private investigator you've been using and give the name to him. See if he can find something out. Try and get some sleep, and I'll see you tomorrow afternoon."

Luke refilled his wine glass and called Josh, his private investigator. "Let me run that name through some channels I have, Luke. If I find something out, do you want me to call you tonight?"

"No matter how late it is, if you find something, I want to know. I've waited so long for this moment I don't want to waste another minute, so yes, whenever you call will be fine."

"Thought you'd say that, Luke. I'll get right on it. Feels good to have something solid after all this time. You okay? You don't sound too good."

"Yeah, man, I'm fine. Think I'm still in shock. I bet I've looked at that locket a million times. Wonder why the darned thing opened now?"

"I have no idea. Guess the time had come. Talk to you later."

Luke walked into the kitchen, knowing he should probably get something in his stomach, but nothing sounded good. He was so tense he was sure he couldn't keep anything down. He emptied his wine glass in the sink and poured himself a glass of water. He looked over at the phone, willing it to ring, but he instinctively knew there was no way Josh could have found anything out this soon.

The next three hours went by from one painful second to the

next. Luke didn't know how many times he'd switched channels on the television or how many times he'd picked up a magazine, flipped through it, and thrown it back in the magazine basket he kept next to his favorite chair. He'd paced from his chair to the outside deck more times than he could count, trying to get rid of his anger. None of it helped. If anything the original ball of fire he'd felt in his stomach had spread throughout his whole body. He was washing his face with cold water when he heard his phone ring. He ran over to it and saw Josh's name on the monitor.

"Yes, Josh. What did you find out?"

"Everything. Your father lives outside a small town called High Desert, not far from Palm Springs. I found several references to him as having one of the finest Native American artifacts collections in the country, but here's the kicker. There are insinuations that some of the things he has aren't legit."

"What do you mean?" Luke asked.

"Means your dad has some items he must have gotten off the black market. Items that could only have been found in caves from which rock art was stolen and things that were dug up from sacred Native American burial grounds."

"Josh, did the information you obtained say how my father could afford to buy those kinds of things? I thought the reason my mother left him was because he was a good-for-nothing. I'm surprised he had money to buy them."

"From the information I got, evidently he found a lode of pure gold. He worked it for a few years and made millions from it. The news articles and the information I got say he lives like a desert rat to cover up the fact that his collection of Native American artifacts is worth millions, and he doesn't want people to know about it."

"Were there any references to my mother or to me?" Luke asked.

"No, none. There was a reference to a woman named Mary

BirdSong. Evidently he lived with her for several years, and they just recently split up. She's a member of the Agua Caliente tribe. You may remember that's the tribe that owns the casino and spa in downtown Palm Springs. Matter of fact the tribe owns half the land in Palm Springs. Tribe members make a lot of money from that. What else do you want me to do?"

"Nothing at the moment. I need to take a day or two to think about this. When I walked in tonight, I never expected all of this. I need to let it settle. I'll call you tomorrow," he said, ending the conversation.

Before he went to bed he took two sleeping pills, but he woke up sometime in the middle of the night troubled by a dream that was as clear to him as if it was happening at that moment. In the dream there was a tomahawk and his father, but the tomahawk was buried in the back of his father's head.

Luke wiped away the cold sweat from his forehead, not knowing if it had been a dream, a nightmare, or a premonition. *Strange,* he thought, *like my father I've collected some very good Native American artifacts, although mine were all bought from reputable dealers in Los Angeles. I wonder if he and I have communicated at some unknown psychic level. I mean why would I collect Native American artifacts, and the father I never knew has a collection of similar items that's worth millions? That's just too strange.*

He got out of bed and walked into his study where several Native American weapons were displayed. He ran his hand over one of them, a tomahawk, and smiled, knowing how he could get rid of the anger he felt.

CHAPTER FIVE

Randy got into his dusty old rusted orange truck which he'd parked at the back of the Hi-Lo lot and drove out to his shack in the hills above the canyon. It was in the canyon where he'd found his first Indian artifacts, artifacts from the Cahuilla Indians. At that time the canyon had been full of them. In the last forty years, it had been pretty much stripped bare of all Native American artifacts after the magazines and newspapers began printing stories about some of the finds that could be made in the canyons around Palm Springs.

When Randy could no longer locate anything worth collecting in the canyons, he turned to black market traders. Those were the people who sold Native American artifacts taken from burial sites and sheets of rocks that had been a canvas for rock art centuries earlier.

He smiled when he saw his old shack and the shed behind it. *No one would ever think some old desert rat like me would have a collection in those two old run-down buildings along with what's in the cave, that's worth millions. Imagine that antique appraiser'll be purty surprised when she sees that stuff.*

Randy parked his truck in the pullout next to the dirt road. He stepped out of his truck and made his way up the footpath to where the shack was located. When he got to the top he walked over to the boulders by his cave, and pressed the number Lucy had given him into his cell phone. Randy knew from years of experience where the best place was to stand on his property so he could successfully place a cell phone call.

"Marty Morgan. May I help you?" the voice on the other end asked.

"Yeah, ya' probably can. Name's Randy Jones. Lucy over at the Hi-Lo's been talkin' ya' up. Says yer' a real hot shot appraiser. I gots a few Injun things I'd like ya' to look at and tell me what they're worth. Any chance ya' could meet me tomorrow at my place? Kind of in a hurry to get this done."

"Yes, Mr. Jones. I believe Lucy mentioned she often developed photographs for a man who collected Indian things. I'm assuming you're that man. I just finished an appraisal yesterday, so your timing is perfect. What time do you want to meet me, and I'll need directions."

They agreed to meet at Randy's shack at noon the next day for a walkthrough, so Marty could get an idea of what items she'd be appraising.

Well, like them fancy talkers would say, 'the die is cast'. S'pose I should call some prospective buyers and let 'em know I'm thinkin' 'bout sellin' all my stuff. Guess I better call Colin and tell him I'd like to see him. When he finds out I wanna sell my stuff, he'll be all over it. Can't say I blame him. It's dang good stuff.

Course the Agua Caliente tribe's pretty wealthy now that they got that casino and spa in town. Rumor has it they could afford to buy about anything. Shoot. Heard they own half the land Palm Springs is sittin' on. Maybe I should call that tribal member, Richard Sagebrush, who says he wants all the collectors to return their Injun things to the rightful owners. Told me once he wanted to honor some relative of his who was their chief in the mid-19th century.

Better not forget 'bout that collector who goes by the name of Dr. Samuel Lowenthal. Everyone knows doctors are rich. Meet him from time to time at shows, and he heard I had some of the really good stuff. Guess the guy lives in some mansion on a golf course.

Probably a good thing I kicked Mary BirdSong out a few months ago. She knew too much. Purty sure she spected' somethin' 'bout my cave, but don't think she ever saw what's in it. I 'member one time catchin' her lookin' at it. That's why I made that special peephole. Lets me see if anyone's around. Anyway, that's where the good stuff is. Hate to show all of it to that appraisal woman, but probably needs to get me somethin' in writin' 'bout my collection's value if I'm gonna sell all of it.

CHAPTER SIX

"This is Colin Sanders, may I help you?"

"Ya' jes' might, Colin, ya' jes' might. This is Randy Jones. Colin, I'm thinkin' 'bout sellin' my stuff. Time to get out of the desert. Been here long enough. Thinkin' the Caribbean sounds good 'bout now. Anyway, got an appraiser comin' tomorrow to set some prices on my stuff. Bought a few pieces from ya' over the years, but as ya' know, I gots a lotta other stuff. Wonderin' if ya'd be interested in buyin' my collection. Want to sell the whole thing at once, not nickel and dime it."

Are you kidding me? Colin thought. *Any dealer in Native American art and artifacts would kill to have the old man's collection. I've been trying for years to figure out a way to get his collection.*

"Of course I'd be interested. I'm pretty familiar with what you have. You even took me to the cave once to show me some of your better things. Why don't you forget about the appraiser? You and I have a very good idea of what the values are for your items. I'll give you a fair price and save you the cost of the appraisal. I could come tomorrow."

"Nah. That won't work. Wanna see what this appraiser says. She doesn't buy or sell the stuff, just appraises it, so she ain't got no dog in the hunt."

"Randy, you're hurting my feelings. I'd give you a fair price, and I'd buy all of your things. Let me take a look at them, and I'll give you a cashier's check for the whole lot and arrange for the items to be packed up and taken away. Only thing you'd have to do is let me look at it and then I'd tell you what I'm willing to pay. You could be finished with the whole thing by tomorrow evening and on your way to the Caribbean."

"That's a dang tempting offer, Colin, but I wanna call a collector I know and let him look at it after I talk to the appraiser. Seen him around at a lot of the shows and know he's a big buyer. Gave me his card and tol' me if I ever wanted to sell my collection, he'd be interested in buyin' it. He's got some mansion at Bighorn Golf Club in Palm Desert. Showed me a picture of it once and that sucker is huge. He's decorated the whole thing with Native American stuff. Tol' me he was thinkin' 'bout building a Native American museum in a few years. Anyway, want him to take a look at my stuff and see if he's interested before I make any decisions."

"All right, Randy, it sounds like your mind is made up. I really would like to have the right of first refusal. We go back a long ways, and I definitely would like to have the chance to buy your collection. I'll wait for your call," Colin said as he ended the conversation.

Wait for his call? Like I'm supposed to hope he'll give me the chance to buy that collection? Fraid not, Randy. I sold you a lot of the items in your collection, things that should never have seen the light of day, and I've been waiting to get my hands on your collection for a long time. All I need is for some sanctimonious collector to go to the authorities and have Randy sing about who sold him his stuff. I'd have to explain a lot of things that might get pretty messy. Even someone who doesn't know much about Native American art would be suspicious when they saw pieces of rock with drawings on them. Wouldn't be much of a stretch for someone to know they were removed from sacred Native American grounds, probably even from caves that were on the reservations.

I'd like to go tonight and convince him, but I've got that meeting with the rich guy from Las Vegas who's coming here just to see me. He told me he specializes in collecting baskets, beaded work, and weapons.

I don't want the appraiser around when I talk to Randy, so I'll wait until tomorrow afternoon after the appraiser has been there, and then I'll pay a little visit to Randy. I might have to do some serious convincing to make him understand that I'm the one who should have his collection. It's about time Randy got rid of his collection. He's old, and he's probably going to die pretty soon anyway. I've never heard him mention children or a wife, so don't think any family members will mourn his death.

Colin walked into the large room in his house where he kept many of his Native American artifacts. He'd carefully arranged pieces he thought would appeal to the buyer he was meeting tonight. He stood looking at them for several minutes then reached down and picked up a tomahawk decorated with eagle feathers. From the number of eagle feathers on it, Colin knew the owner had been a high-ranking warrior, maybe even a chief, at least that's how he'd intended to sell it.

Might just give this tomahawk to Randy as a present and tell him he can have it along with the money. Big bucks will never miss it. Matter of fact, he'll never even know it was supposed to be part of what I'm going to show him, but it sure might come in handy when I go see Randy.

He smiled, but the smile never reached his cold eyes. On Colin, a turned up mouth was so rare that it almost hurt him to smile. One didn't make a fortune dealing in Native American black market artifacts by being a nice guy, but he had a fleeting thought of how fitting it would be for Randy to die from a tomahawk blow to his head, and he couldn't help but smile.

That would give a new meaning to the term "burying the hatchet," Colin giggled as he took the tomahawk to his office and put it aside for tomorrow's meeting with Randy. *Maybe it's just as well that my new client doesn't see it. Who knows? It could be a federal sting operation and almost everybody knows that possessing eagle feathers is illegal, plus I really don't want to get into a lot of explanations. No, it's far more fitting to confront Randy with an illegal Native American item.*

CHAPTER SEVEN

Dr. Samuel Lowenthal stood in front of the framed war bonnet he'd just hung in his living room and admired it. He'd carefully positioned it over the cream-colored couch, so that the brilliant colors in the bonnet were the focal point of the off-white wall. When Dr. Sam, as he preferred to be called by his orthopedic patients, had finally convinced his mother to let him display the Great Plains war bonnet that had been in the family for almost a century, he was thrilled. It was a piece that commanded the attention of everyone who saw it. Intricately decorated with beadwork, ribbons, and thirty-three feathers from three golden eagles, it was stunningly beautiful.

He realized how fortunate his family was to even have it. The sale of war bonnets with feathers from eagles had been outlawed since the 1960's. The one Dr. Sam had just hung was given to his great-great-grandfather by a tribal chief in Montana in exchange for medical treatment he'd provided free of charge to members of the chief's tribe over a period of several years.

Dr. Sam looked around his house and smiled, as he admired the different pieces he'd collected and displayed in his large home on the golf course. When he hired the interior designer to decorate his home, he'd been very clear that she was to use a neutral palette for the furniture, walls, and floors. Dr. Sam wanted his Native American artifacts to be the focal point of the house.

He regretted that his collection lacked any really fine Pre-Columbian pottery such as bowls, ollas, and unique Native American baskets. He had a few pieces of each of them, but when he'd found very good, one-of-a-kind pieces, they weren't in perfect condition. Dr. Sam wanted only the best for his collection and was prepared to pay whatever it took to obtain them. The problem was, he couldn't find them.

Lately he'd been waking up in the middle of the night obsessing about the pieces he wanted to add to his collection. He'd been in contact with a number of antique dealers who specialized in Native American items, but none of them had been able to find exactly what he wanted. He knew it wasn't healthy to be obsessing about something he might never be able to obtain. Even though he'd always considered himself to be mentally healthy, he was beginning to have second doubts. He kept having a recurring dream where he was murdering a man who had the pieces he wanted. His rational side couldn't believe he'd even dreamt something like that. Dr. Sam's dark side had started surfacing with the dream. It was getting to the point where his dark side was willing to do anything to get the pieces he wanted, including murder.

His phone rang, breaking his reverie. He looked at the monitor and didn't recognize the number. "Dr. Sam Lowenthal. May I help you?"

"Jes' might, Doc. This here's Randy Jones. Met ya' at a coupla Indian shows around these parts. I'm the one who tol' ya' I had better Anasazi pottery and baskets than we was seein' at the shows."

"Why, yes, I do remember you. As I recall, I believe you told me you were a collector with a number of high quality items in your collection."

"That be right. Probably have one of the best collections that's in private hands. Anyway, thinkin' of sellin' it. Thought I'd give you a call and see if you got any interest in buyin' it. Woman's comin' here tomorrow who's an appraiser. Gonna show her the stuff, and she's gonna write me up a report 'bout what it's worth. Got a coupla other people who wanna see it. Any chance you'd like to have your name added to the list, cuz I could make time for ya' tomorrow afternoon, so ya' could take a looksee and tell me if ya' got any interest."

"Just a moment, let me look at my schedule." He walked over to his computer and pulled up his schedule for the following day. "I have a couple of appointments in the afternoon, but I can easily cancel them. Would you be willing to sell me a few pieces, or are you thinking of selling your whole collection to just one buyer?"

"Don't want to mess around with it. Getting' a hankerin' to go to the Caribbean for a little fun in the sun if ya' know what I mean. Ain't breakin' up the collection. Take me too long to sell it piecemeal. Want someone to buy the whole shebang."

"Well, I see no reason why that can't be arranged if I'm interested in the pieces."

"Doc, yer' gonna be interested in the pieces. You can take that to the bank. Ya' see what I got, and ya' won't ever have to look for any more pieces. I gots the best of the best."

"Good. I'm looking forward to it. Please give me your address, and I probably better have your phone number as well."

"Ain't got no address, leastways not one ya' could find on one of them computer maps. Here's how to get to my place."

A few minutes later, after he'd taken down the directions to Randy's shack, Dr. Sam sat with his elbows on his desk, chin in his hands.

If Randy Jones really does have the pieces I want, and I don't think he'd call me about them if he didn't, I'll have to buy the whole collection, and I have no idea what's in it or how many pieces there are, and that's not to mention the cost of buying the entire collection when I only want very specific types of pieces. The cost of the entire collection could be in the hundreds of thousands of dollars, even millions. Although I'm wealthy, I simply don't have that kind of money. Of course one alternative is I could just kill him and take the pieces I want. Make it a lot simpler. Then I wouldn't even have to buy the entire collection, or that matter, even have to buy the pieces I need.

Good grief. I can't believe that thought even went through my mind. Maybe I should make an appointment with the psychiatrist who's on staff at the Medical Center. I feel like there's a dark side of me that's becoming stronger and stronger. Me? A murderer?

"Yeah," a voice inside his head said. "You could kill him with one of those tomahawks in your collection. No one would ever suspect a mild-mannered doctor, and you'd have what we want. I'll help you."

CHAPTER EIGHT

Richard Sagebrush had been visiting a friend near High Desert when he realized he needed a few things, and decided the Hi-Lo Drug Store was as good a place to buy them as anywhere. He was standing at the checkout counter when Mary BirdSong approached him and said, "Richard, I need to talk to you. Can you tell me a time that would be convenient for you?"

"I have some time right now, if that works for you, Mary."

"Yes, please follow me out to the parking lot. We can sit in my truck and talk."

Richard followed her out to her truck and got in on the passenger side. Although they both were members of the Agua Caliente tribe and received large monthly stipends from the casino money the tribe earned, they'd both lived at a poverty level for most of their lives. They were reluctant to spend their newly found bonanza of money, instead investing it in stocks and mutual funds. Many other tribal members spent every cent of their monthly allotment on whatever caught their fancy, and a lot of it went towards alcohol and drugs. It wasn't uncommon to see a brand new truck in front of a dilapidated trailer that was about to collapse in the next winter storm.

The upside of the new wealth that had come to a number of the tribes in California when the tribal gaming compact had been ratified in 1999 was that not only were the tribal members wealthy, but the extra money had allowed the tribes to build state-of-the-art schools on their reservations as well as medical facilities to match. The tribes generally paid all of the college costs for tribal members who wanted to get a higher education. Psychologists were now on the medical staffs as the tribes tried to find ways to deal with the rampant abuse of alcohol and drugs as well as with problems of spousal abuse.

The downside of the new wealth was that people had little reason to go to college. They knew that each month they would get a large check. The new wealth allowed for even more abuse of alcohol and drugs, as many of the tribal members who received them saw no need to work. The money from the casino was a double-edged sword, with the winners often being local car dealers, liquor stores, and drug dealers.

Mary and Richard wanted to retain as much of their tribal culture as possible for future generations. Both of them had worked hard to help the younger generation learn the Cahuilla language by teaching it through the bird songs which both of them had learned as young children. The songs also told legends about the origin of the Cahuilla tribe. In 1990 only thirty-five people had spoken the language, but through Mary's and Richard's dedication to helping their tribe, many now spoke the language. Obviously, Mary had been named for the tradition by her father who often sang the bird songs at tribal gatherings.

Richard had been part of a coalition that had gone to Sacramento, California, and later to Washington, D.C., working to have objects that been stolen from tribal burial sites or other sacred places repatriated to the tribe from which the objects had been stolen. He was a nationally recognized authority on the topic of stolen Native American artifacts, and he spoke to Native Americans throughout the United States on the subject. Some people considered him to be fanatic about the subject.

"Well, Mary, what did you want to talk to me about?" he asked.

She ran her hands over the truck's steering wheel and then wiped them on her jeans. "Richard, this is difficult for me. I guess I better start at the beginning. Several years ago I met a man named Randy Jones in a bar outside of town called the Road Runner Bar. Richard, don't look at me like that. I rarely drink any more, but once in a while I used to go in there. We got to know each other, and one thing led to another. He asked me to move in with him, and against the wishes of my family and other tribal members, I did."

"I know Randy Jones, and I'm well aware you lived with him. No one in the tribe could understand it, particularly since a lot of people know he's a big collector of our sacred artifacts. Some say he has things that are illegal. Maybe you'd know about that."

She brushed a piece of hair off her forehead. No one would ever consider her to be an attractive woman. She was heavy and had a thick body along with a pock-marked face from the acne she had as a young woman. Her complexion was sallow and she looked much older than her age. The years of drinking had taken its toll on her lined face. Mary held up her hand. "Please, let me continue. When you get to be my age, and no one has ever wanted you for a wife, or pretty much anything else, you get a little desperate. Okay, maybe very desperate. Anyway, he was good to me and remember, this was before the tribe had any money. I moved into his small shack and lived with him until a few months ago."

"What happened?"

"I don't know. He came back from the bar one night and told me to get out. He said it was over, and he didn't want anything more to do with me. I think maybe he was worried I'd found out about the cave where he keeps the special pieces of his Indian artifacts collection, the ones no one ever sees."

"I'm at a loss here, Mary. What are you talking about?"

She gulped several times and continued, "Randy has all kinds of things that he must have gotten on the black market hidden in a cave near his shack. I watched him go there one day, and he moved two rocks that were in front of a small opening on a large rocky hill. I was fascinated by what he was doing. He must have done it a lot of times before then, but maybe it had been when I was at work. When I was sure the tribal money wasn't going away, I quit working, so I was at the shack a lot more.

"Anyway, he moved the rocks, and I saw there was a door he must have built that opened into a cave. I saw him walk into it. He was in there for about an hour. When he came out he put the rocks back and walked back to the shack. I pretended like I was making some fry bread for dinner. Although he didn't say anything, I wonder if he looked out of a peephole or something in the cave and saw me watching. I don't know."

"Did you ever see what was in the cave?" Richard asked.

She swallowed nervously and said, "Yes. He went to town a few days later, and I went in it. I couldn't believe what I saw. There were sheets of rock art, headdresses, weapons, baskets, pottery, and all kinds of things. I've never seen Native American objects like that, even in the museums. Richard, almost everything in there was illegal. None of it could have been bought in a store or at an auction. I know how hard you've fought for repatriation, and I've struggled with myself for several months about whether or not to tell you what I saw in that cave. I don't know what can be done about it, but when I woke up this morning I knew I had to tell you. For the sake of the tribe, I had to tell you."

Richard's face became flushed with anger, and he started breathing heavily. "Tell me where the cave is, Mary. I'd go out there right now, but I have a meeting in an hour, and I'm tied up tomorrow until late afternoon. I'll go then. I want you to draw me a map of exactly where the cave is located."

She took a notepad from her purse and drew a map for him. When she was finished she handed it to him and said, "In many ways Randy's a good man. I know he smokes and drinks too much, so his health may not be so good. A few months before I left he started coughing a lot. I know how important this is to you, and I felt I had to tell you about it." Mary said as she started crying.

"You did the right thing, Mary. You don't need to worry about it anymore. Thanks, and I'll let you know what happens after I talk to him." He reached over and patted her arm and then opened the passenger door.

Richard got into his truck, becoming angrier by the minute. He was tired of the waiting. The courts, the Bureau of Indian Affairs, and the Bureau of Land Management all moved too slowly, if at all. It was usually years before something happened, before he could get the sacred items back in the hands of the tribe to whom they belonged. If there were a lot of things in the cave, and Mary had certainly led him to believe there were, he might not even live long enough to see them returned to their rightful owners.

Maybe it's time I took justice into my own hands. What right does that man have to possess the sacred items of my tribe and others as well? As long as there are buyers like him, there will always be people willing to desecrate our sacred lands. He's an old man. I'd probably be doing everybody a favor by getting rid of him. I've never done anything like this in my life, but I'm tired of working so hard and still having to stand hopelessly by as our sacred sites are raped. It's wrong. I can always say someone donated the illegal items anonymously to the tribe. No one will have to know where they came from. Mary might, but she won't say anything. Be pretty fitting if he was killed by something made and used by Native Americans, like a tomahawk. And I know where to find one.

He drove to his modest home on the Agua Caliente Reservation which was right in the middle of Palm Springs thinking how wonderful it would be to recover his tribe's and other tribe's sacred objects. Richard had discovered his calling early in his life and if the calling involved murder, so be it.

CHAPTER NINE

The morning after she got back from her trip to Chicago, Marty and Duke were walking by Laura's house just as she stepped out with a cup of coffee in her hand. "Welcome back. How was Chicago?"

"Terrific. I'll tell you all about it later. Right now I have a dog that needs to commune with nature. See you in a few minutes."

Laura kneeled down and scratched Duke's ear. "Glad I don't have to do the bootie bit anymore, big guy. Mama's home, and I have to tell you I felt like a fool walking around with some huge black dog wearing pink booties." She looked up at Marty. "Maybe it's time to see if you can dispense with the booties."

"Don't think so. I tried before I left, so you wouldn't have to put them on, but he stood perfectly still and absolutely refused to have anything to do with the desert floor without his booties. Trust me, if that big boy doesn't want to move, it's not going to happen."

"I'd like to talk to you for a minute when you get back," Laura said. "I'm going to drink my coffee in the courtyard and check my messages. Want a cup? I've got plenty."

"Love it. Oh, good morning, John. You're up early," she said to the resident chef who was also the owner of The Red Pony food truck.

"Yeah. Some office put in a large order for panini sandwiches. I need to assemble them and get The Red Pony down to the Springs, so I can grill them and keep them warm. They placed an order for forty of them. It's going to take a while to do them on my grill. I'm off to pick up Max. He's going to help me. Oh, by the way, I'm trying out a noodle paella tonight. I've never made it before, and it may be way too much trouble for the Pony, but we'll see how it goes. Looked interesting when I read about it in one of the food magazines. I imagine your detective friend will be here for dinner, Marty. Would I be right?"

"Probably, although I haven't talked to him since I got back. I'll give him a call later on and invite him. He's one of your biggest fans, and I'm sure he won't want to miss the paella. Good luck today," she said, as she walked through the gate with Duke.

When they returned a few minutes later Marty said, "Laura, can you give me a couple of minutes more? I need to feed Duke, and then I'm all yours."

"Sure. I still have a little time before I have to start getting ready for work."

"Okay, Laura," Marty said a few minutes later as she sat down at the large picnic table that was the central focus of the courtyard and was surrounded by the four communal style homes. "I'm all yours. What did you want to talk to me about?"

"Well, I hate to butt into your life, but you know sometimes I get special feelings or whatever you want to call them."

"Somehow I don't think I'm going to like what I'm going to hear in the next few minutes. I well remember when you had the feeling about where the lost diamond ring was at that appraisal I was doing at Mrs. Jensen's home. Since she'd been murdered and couldn't tell us where she'd hidden the ring your whatever you want to call it took over and found it. I have to tell you though, when you sliced the styrofoam wig stand open with that butcher knife, and the ring popped out, I think you took ten years off of my friend Carl's life.

Matter of fact, I've noticed he avoids me at the monthly antique appraiser meetings. I have to admit that was pretty spectacular," she said laughing.

"Marty," Laura said becoming serious, "I had a dream last night about you. It involved some Native American things and a tomahawk. I couldn't tell exactly what it was about, but I had the feeling you were going to be in danger. Does any of this make sense to you? Are you involved in some appraisal concerning Native American artifacts?"

"Nope. I'm kind of surprised I haven't been asked to do an appraisal of that type here in the desert. Certainly seems like those things fit in with the desert a lot more than some of the European and early American items I've recently appraised. Actually, I know quite a bit about those types of artifacts, but I haven't made use of it here. I did several appraisals of Native American artifacts when I was living in the Midwest before Scott and I got divorced, so I'd enjoy using what I learned. I just haven't been asked."

"I know it's not much to go on Marty, but if you find yourself doing something with Native American artifacts, be careful. Maybe that's the message. You need to be careful. I have a feeling you're going to be involved in something to do with those types of objects, and it's going to be soon. My alarm bells are starting to go off."

"Swell. That's just the way I want to start my day out. You telling me your alarm bells are going off."

"Marty, I know how you hate for me to say this, but I can tell that what I just said made you nervous. Your right eyelid is twitching."

"I am not nervous. My eyelid's just telling me it didn't get enough sleep last night. That's all it is."

"Right. You can fool everyone else about your nervous twitch, but you can't fool me. I remember when we were kids, and you were afraid that mom or dad would find out you'd done something you shouldn't. They always knew you'd done something bad because your eyelid would start twitching."

I'd like to throw this cup of coffee in my dear big mouth sister's face, but the scream would probably wake Les up, and I know he needs his sleep. Good grief, I'm a grown woman about to celebrate my fiftieth birthday, and that darned eyelid is still giving me away. I wonder if I'll ever outgrow it.

"So, Marty, what's on your agenda today?" Laura asked, deftly changing the subject from what she knew inflamed her sister.

"I need to do a lot of research on the Tiffany pieces I saw in Chicago. The identification of them wasn't hard for me, but it's going to take a bit of work to find out what they're worth. Some of them are really rare, and that makes it even harder. A lot of it's just a judgment call on my part. I also have to go into town and get the photos I took in Chicago from Lucy at the Hi-Lo. Need anything in town?"

"No, I think I'm good." Laura looked at her watch. "Love to sit here and talk to you some more, but it's time for me to get my act together and look presentable for work. See you tonight." She stood up, turned, and walked into her house.

"Come on Duke, let's go call Jeff. He should be at work by now."

Jeff was Detective Jeff Combs with the Palm Springs Police Department. She'd met him when she'd appraised the estate of a woman who had been murdered, and it had been Jeff's case. There had been an instant attraction between the good-looking middle-aged detective and the attractive appraiser, and the relationship had grown from there, although neither one of them was quite ready to commit to marriage.

A few minutes later she heard a warm masculine voice on the other end of the phone say, "I missed you, Marty. I'm glad you're back. It's lonesome here without you."

"I'll bet you say that to all the women you know," she said in a teasing voice. "In a town like Palm Springs, attractive single women are a dime a dozen."

"That may be true, but they're not you. Speaking of which, when can I see you?"

"John's making noodle paella tonight, and he specifically invited you. Actually, Jeff, I missed you, too."

"Knew I'd get you to admit I'm creeping under your skin. It's just a matter of time, and you'll be all mine."

"Or vice-versa. I definitely feel a deep attraction to you. Beyond that I don't know."

Jeff laughed. "Well, I guess that's a good start, but it sounds like you're not quite ready to invite me to the compound for good."

"Not quite, but I won't absolutely rule it out for the future."

"A man can live with hopeful words like that. Gotta go, I'm late for a meeting. See you around six tonight. Loves."

She hung up, shaking her head. *He's incorrigible. After Scott, I never thought I'd want to get into a serious relationship, but it sure looks like I'm heading for one, and I don't seem to be putting up much of a fight.*

CHAPTER TEN

Marty spent the morning and the early afternoon pouring through auction catalogs, reference books, and on the Internet looking for replacement prices she could put on the Tiffany pieces. In many cases, they were one-of-a-kind items, so there weren't any comparables available. Items with no comparables were the ones that always worried Marty when she did an appraisal. It became a judgment call, her judgment call, and one she sincerely hoped was never questioned.

She looked at the time of day displayed on the bottom of her computer screen and realized the day had gotten away from her. She just had time to go into town, pick up the Chicago appraisal photographs from Lucy, and make it back in time to get ready for dinner.

"Come on Duke, let's go for a ride." With those magic words the dog turned himself into a pretzel. He walked to the gate with Marty but then came to a complete stop.

"Duke, come on, you can walk to my car without your booties on. It's just a few steps." He looked up at her as if to say, "There is no way I am putting one paw on that desert floor."

"All right, you win, but this is ridiculous," she said as he accompanied her back to her house to get the booties. She slipped them on and he eagerly walked over to her car, wagging his tail, and waiting for her to open the door. As soon as he was in, she reached over and removed the booties. The people in the compound knew he wore booties and so did Jeff, but that was where it ended. She was still a newcomer in the little redneck town of High Desert, and she could only imagine what would be said about her if people found out her big black male dog wore pink booties.

The Hi-Lo parking lot was full. It seemed to be a day when everyone needed something from the Hi-Lo. She rolled down all of the windows in the car and made sure Duke had some water in his dish. One of the things she'd learned early on in the desert was how hot a car could get when left in the sun with the windows rolled up. Since it was very early spring and relatively cool, she felt okay about leaving him in the car, something she would never think of doing in summer or early fall. As she opened the door to the drugstore she was immediately greeted by Lucy.

"Hey, lady. Them Tiffany pictures are somethin' else. Saw an ad fer the museum in LA on the tube one time 'bout them havin' some exhibit on Tiffany lamps. From what I saw in yer' photos, looks like that guy had more good stuff than he could say grace over."

Marty smiled at Lucy's way with words. "It was a fun one to do. I don't expect to ever see that many superb Tiffany pieces again. I'm glad I was able to do it. What's that?" Marty asked, looking down at a notepad in front of Lucy with something written on it.

Lucy looked down at the piece of paper. "Did I ever tell ya' I do a thought for the day? Trying' to be a better person and all. Wanna hear my thought fer today?"

"Yes, that would be nice. Good for you for doing it. So, what's your thought for the day?"

Lucy picked up the piece of paper and read, "If you're worried, it's because you're living in a time other than the present moment." Lucy looked up at Marty. "So whaddya think? Good words?"

"Yes, I think there's probably a lot of truth in them. Problem is, we tend to forget things like that when we need them the most and they could do the best good."

"Sure 'nuf, ain't no slack in that rope. Was out at the Road Runner last Saturday and instead of me and Luke just enjoyin' ourselves, I kept thinkin' 'bout that husband I kicked outta the house years ago. Waste of time on my part. Dunno why I was even thinkin' 'bout him. Haven't had nothin' to do with him fer years. Ya' know, sometimes them thoughts jes' creep up on ya'."

"Yes. I know what you mean. You're not the only one with an ex-husband who jumps into one's thoughts from time to time."

"Knew ya'd understand. We're kinda whaddya call it, kinder spirits or somethin' like that."

"Think you mean kindred spirits."

"Ya', that's what I said. Kinder spirits. Here's yer' purties. Oh, by the way, 'member me tellin' ya' 'bout that guy that's got all them Injun things?"

"Vaguely. Why?"

"His name's Randy Jones, and he was in earlier today and asked me to give him yer' phone number. Said he was gonna call ya' and have ya' appraise his Injun stuff."

Marty felt a cold stab fear race through her body. All she could think of was the conversation she'd had a few hours earlier with her sister about Native American artifacts and the danger of doing an appraisal of them.

Laura's uncanny. How could she possibly know that someone was going to call me and ask me to do an appraisal of Native American artifacts? Well, maybe she's wrong this time.

"Thanks, Lucy. Anything else go on while I was gone?"

"Nah, things were pretty quiet. Had some purty boy in here

yesterday drivin' some big black fancy Cadillac askin' 'bout Randy. Sure couldn't figger out why he'd wanna see Randy. Nothin' 'bout him looked like he was from around these parts."

"Thanks, Lucy. Well, I better get home and match these photos up with what I was working on today, so I can send it to the woman who types up my appraisal reports for me. See you around."

"Back at ya'. Lookin' forward to seein' them photos from Randy's stuff. Have a feelin' he's got stuff I ain't never seen. Tell everybody at the compound hi for me."

"Will do." Marty said as she opened the drugstore door. As usual Duke was sitting in the passenger seat of the car, looking towards where he'd last seen her when she'd entered the drugstore. When he saw her come out the door, he stood up, his big tail swishing from side to side.

"I'm back, big guy. Let's go home."

I can't get the conversation with Laura out of my mind. I wonder if that's the Native American things Laura was talking about this morning. From what Lucy's told me, it sounds like this guy has some pretty spectacular stuff. Anyway, if he should call me, I do think I'd like to see his collection. I can always make a decision about taking on the assignment later. Time to go home and give Jeff a reason to be interested in me.

CHAPTER ELEVEN

Marty had just walked out the door of her home when the gate leading to the compound opened and Detective Jeff Combs walked in. She ran over to him and hugged him, not caring who saw her. They kissed passionately, but Jeff had to step away when Duke began to bark. Although Duke tolerated Jeff, he apparently decided that this particular kiss had lasted far too long, plus he wanted the dog cookie Jeff always kept in his pocket for him.

"If I can get a welcome like this every time you come back after being gone for a few days, maybe you better do more out-of-town appraisals." He reached in his pocket and pulled out Duke's dog treat. "Here you go, Duke. I know this is what you want. I'd like to resume where I left off with that kiss, but I get the distinct impression from Duke's reaction that isn't going to happen," he said laughing.

They walked over to where the others were already seated at the picnic table in the center of the courtyard, greeting John and his assistant Max, Les, and Laura. "Sit down, Jeff. We're having a glass of wine before I get serious with this noodle paella I'm going to make. Once I start, I can't hold it. One of my teachers once told me that pasta waits for no man, and I don't think any truer words have ever been spoken," John said.

"It's good to be here. John, I really missed your cooking while

Marty was back in Chicago. I'm trying to get Marty to let me move in permanently, but I'm encountering some resistance," Jeff said, looking at her.

"I really don't think this is a subject that needs to be discussed publicly," Marty said, blushing. "I just need a little more time."

"Well, I'd like to put my two cents in," Les said. "I think I speak for all of us when I say you'd be welcome here when Marty finally makes up her mind."

"Thanks for the vote of confidence. I appreciate it, but I think Marty holds the power here, so I guess I'll just continue to enjoy the dinners and the company."

"I'm going to change the subject," Marty said. "Laura, remember the conversation we had this morning about the Native American things? Well, guess what? I got a call today from a man who wants me to appraise his Native American artifacts collection. He says it's really good. I'm going out to his, as he calls it, shack, tomorrow and he's going to show me what he wants appraised."

Laura put her hand on her chest and with an alarmed look on her face said, "Marty, I really don't have a good feeling about this. Why don't you call him back and cancel? I have nothing to base it on, just a gut feeling."

Jeff turned to Laura and said, "I'm in the dark here, and the others may be, too. Could you fill us in?"

Laura told them about the dream she'd had the night before and her conversation this morning with Marty. "Since we talked this morning, my feelings have intensified, and I really wish you wouldn't go out there tomorrow," she said as she looked intently at Marty.

"You made a believer out of me, Laura, when you helped Marty with the Jensen appraisal. If it hadn't been for you, I'm not sure I ever could have solved the crime and figured out who murdered Mrs. Jensen." He turned to Marty. "I agree with Laura. If she has a bad feeling about it, I wish you'd pass on this one. If there's even a chance that something could happen, I'd rather you didn't do it."

"I wish all of you would quit trying to decide what I should and shouldn't do, from letting Jeff move in to telling me which appraisals I should go on. I really like seeing good Native American pieces, and from what I understand from this collector, it promises to be a superb collection. I've made up my mind to go and that's that."

There was silence in the courtyard for several long moments and then Jeff spoke. "All right, I can certainly see where someone who appreciates really fine Native American artifacts would want to see what's in the collection, but I would ask one thing of you."

"What's that?"

"I'm off tomorrow, and I'd like to go with you. It would make me feel a lot better if you'd say yes."

"Jeff, I can't do that. There's a confidentiality issue here. The collector asked me to come. He didn't ask me to bring someone with me. That would be totally inappropriate, but I will make you a promise."

"Swell. Can't wait to hear what it is," he said sarcastically.

"I'll carry my cell phone with me. If there's even a hint that something isn't right, I'll call you. I'll even go one step better. If I feel threatened or think something is wrong, I'll leave, and I won't do the appraisal. I think that's a very fair compromise."

"I don't think compromises count when your life could be in jeopardy, but I've learned one thing. If you're dead set on doing or not doing something, that's what's going to happen. Anyway, I'll have my phone with me, and I'll be there as soon as I can if you call me. Where is it? I'd like to be somewhat nearby and not stuck in Palm Springs traffic in case you call."

"It's a few miles outside of High Desert, literally in the desert near a canyon. Thanks for understanding. I appreciate it."

"Okay, everybody, now that we've worked out the details of the appraisal Marty's going on tomorrow, I think we better have some sustenance. Max, it's time for us to shine in the kitchen. Everything's prepped, so it shouldn't take more than a half an hour. Can't wait to hear what you think about this dish," John said as he got up and motioned for Max to follow him.

After the two men left, Marty told the others about the appraisal she'd just conducted in Chicago and the "idiot savant."

"I'm glad you mentioned it, Marty," Laura said. "I was talking to Dick today about it, and he said that the man's personal assistant was so happy with the work you did and your professionalism he wanted to set up a time for you to appraise the items in his house here in the desert. Dick told me it would probably take a couple of days. He's going to call you tomorrow."

"Great. The client has a wonderful eye, and I think he's acquired some of the best of the best. If you talk to Dick before I do, please be sure and tell him that I definitely want to do it. Thanks."

A half hour later John walked into the courtyard carrying a large bowl with steam coming out of it. Max followed with a green salad in a glass bowl and bread sticks. "Time for noodle paella. I've never before had it or made it, so you're definitely guinea pigs. I came across it in a food magazine, and it caught my eye. As always, I want you to be truthful." He put the bowl on the table and served some of the paella to each of them in smaller bowls. Max passed the salad around. Everyone was quiet for a few minutes as they sampled the new dish.

Laura was the first one to break the silence. "John, this is not only fabulous, it's beautiful as well. What's in it?"

"Shrimp, clams, chicken, and Italian sausage. What I think's interesting is how the red pepper, the leek, and the parsley give it texture and color. Of course there are some other things in it, but those are the basics. I've made paella a number of times, and I've always used wine and chicken broth. This called for clam juice and diced tomatoes. The spaghetti cooks in the juices rather than in a separate pan, and I think it works even better than the traditional way of cooking pasta. What do you think?"

"From how fast this is disappearing from everyone's bowl, I think you have a huge hit here. I'd like another serving. The paella I've had before had rice in it, and I think the noodles make it even better, but then again I'm a pasta freak. I've never met a noodle I didn't like," Jeff said.

"Me too," John said. "That's probably what appealed to me in the first place, plus I was fascinated by cooking the noodles in clam broth and tomatoes. That's a first for me. I've got one little problem. I just don't know if it would be as good if I kept it warm and served it at The Red Pony. I think I'll have to try it again and see how it is after it's been held for a couple of hours, because there's no way I could make it fresh and serve it. It would take longer than my customers' lunch hour."

An hour later John looked at the empty paella bowl and said, "Probably a good thing I didn't make dessert. Since you ate every bit of it, even if you had a dessert pocket in your stomach, I think that would be full too," he said, laughing. "Glad you liked it. It's fun to cook for such an appreciative group."

"Trust me, the pleasure is all ours. I never knew when you rented this house from me, that I'd be having gourmet meals every night, courtesy of my new tenant," Laura said.

"I'm hardly a new tenant. I think living here ten years qualifies me as an old-timer."

"All right. I'll amend that to courtesy of an old-timer."

"Thank you. Max and I need to clean up and get some sleep. That office staff liked the panini sandwiches so much they ordered them again for tomorrow. Not complaining, mind you, just want to make sure I'm bright-eyed and bushy-tailed in the morning."

"I need to go, too," Jeff said. "Even though I'm off tomorrow there's a case I'm working on that needs some Internet attention. Marty, see me to the door?"

She stood up and they walked to the gate and out to his car. Duke didn't have his booties on, so he stayed at the gate, watching them.

"I think I've discovered how I can have a little time with you alone. From now on we'll walk outside the gate, and he'll have to stay in there," Jeff said grinning as he wrapped his arms around her. "I really wasn't kidding about wanting to live here with you. If you're not comfortable with that, you're always welcome to move into my condo. Of course I don't know what Duke would do there, and I sure wouldn't want to be seen with him outside in his pink booties. That would be your job,"

"A little more time, Jeff, give me a little more…" His kiss stopped her words and for once, she had nothing to say. She was simply doing what Lucy had talked about earlier that day, "Being in the moment."

CHAPTER TWELVE

Marty spent the next morning researching and reviewing in a general manner, all sorts of Native American artifacts. The beauty of the pieces created by tribal people never failed to touch her. These were items which had transcended their utilitarian purpose and become highly coveted treasures by those who collected them. She was really looking forward to seeing Randy Jones' collection.

As she was casually doing the research, she thought once again how lucky she and her sister had been to inherit their mother's good genes. Her tanned face was relatively unlined and large brown eyes were an accent to the auburn hair which framed her face. At 5'3" she was short, so she always packed a stepstool when she went on an appraisal in case she needed it to reach items in high places. A well-rounded hourglass figure complemented her attractive appearance. She thought she'd pass inspection from an old desert rat. Although her fiftieth birthday was only weeks away, she could still pass for being in her early forties.

Her meeting with Randy was scheduled for 2:00 that afternoon. At 1:30 she put her appraisal tools in the trunk of her car: notebook, pen, camera, small stepstool, flashlight, and white and black fabric material in case she decided to start the appraisal today and needed a background to photograph smaller items. Around her neck she wore a heavy gold chain attached to a magnifying glass surrounded by gold filigree with diamond insets. Even though her ex-husband Scott had given it to her as a piece of jewelry, and she really didn't want or need reminders of him, it was so easy to wear it around her neck and it kept her hands free.

Marty double-checked to make sure the clothes she was wearing were appropriate for appraising items in a shack, a shed, and a cave, whatever that meant. Although the jeans and tennis shoes she wore wouldn't have been suitable for the appraisal she'd just conducted in Chicago, Marty decided if she was going to be looking at items in a cave, her outfit would be just fine. She wore a crisp white blouse and even though it was warm, she put a jacket in the car. The weather had a way of changing quickly in the desert.

She followed the directions Randy had given her and soon saw the shack and shed ahead of her on the right. He'd told her to park in the turnout next to his orange truck. When she stepped out of her car she saw the narrow footpath that led up the slope of a ridge to the shack. The path gently sloped upwards, and she was able to easily walk up it.

When she reached the top of the path she saw that the door to the shack was open, allowing a light breeze to pass through it. In the muted interior light of the shack she saw a grizzled old man with a cigarette dangling from his lips and a full white beard. His worn blue denim shirt and jeans, along with old scuffed cowboy boots, made him look like a caricature from a western movie.

He stood up when he saw her shadow coming through the open door and said, "You must be Marty Morgan. I'm Randy Jones, but you probably knew that. Come on in. I'll show ya' some of my purties here and in the shed before we go to the cave. That's where I keep the real good stuff."

She walked into the shack and stood dumbfounded. Randy hadn't been kidding when he said he had a good collection. He may have looked like a caricature of a desert rat, but within that grizzled old man was the eye of a collector who just might be one of the most astute she'd ever been around.

"Randy, would you mind if I just take a few minutes and look at these things? I'd also like to take some notes, and then you can tell me more about them when I actually do the appraisal. I'd also like to take a few photographs, so I can do a little research before the appraisal."

"Nah, take yer' time. Got a couple of people coming out later this afternoon to look at my purties, but fer right now I'm all yers'."

Marty slowly walked around the small shack trying to process what she was seeing. She couldn't believe there could possibly be any better Native American pieces in the cave than what she was seeing. Beaded belts, rugs, pottery, baskets, and other artifacts filled the tiny shack. It was obvious Randy had either traveled extensively or bought pieces from dealers, because most of the items were not indigenous to the tribes of the desert area.

She turned to him and said, "Mr. Jones, you have some of the best things I've ever seen. I feel like I'm in a museum, and I'm the only person allowed in. This collection alone is priceless. How long have you been collecting Native American artifacts?"

"Well, let's see," he said putting his cigarette out in an empty can of beans that doubled as an ashtray and was overflowing with cigarette butts, while at the same time lighting another cigarette. "Started some thirty-five years ago or so. Had a little luck with a mother lode of gold, and one thing kinda led to another."

"You mentioned something about selling your collection. Do you have a buyer for it, or are you going to sell pieces to collectors who might just want to buy the pottery, say."

"Nah. I'm sellin' the whole kit and caboodle. Goin' to the Caribbean and figger won't do me no good there. Got two people who are gonna be lookin' at it. One's a hot shot bone doctor who collects high-end Injun stuff. He's comin' out here later to look at my purties. Also got a dealer who's sold me some of 'em, so he's got a purty good idea of what I got. Problem is Colin's cheap. Don't know if he'll pay what I'm gonna ask for it, course that depends on what ya' think it's worth."

"It's none of my business, but what about gifting your collection to a museum? In my opinion pieces of this quality should be available for everyone to see."

"Nah, want the money. Anyway, don't think I'll be around long enough to use the tax break I'd get. Uncle Sam ain't got no idea what I got here and don't want him to find out about it. Try to stay off the grid as much as I can, and I been purty dang good at it."

"I don't mean to pry, but what about your family? I'm thinking your children might want these items."

"Jes' might. Only got one kid and ain't seen him for forty years, so don't think it matters much to him. Matter a fact, don't even know where he is. Sure as heck hasn't tried to find me. Now if yer' finished jawin' at me, like to show ya' what's in the shed, and then we'll go to the cave."

"That's fine. Could you give me a couple of minutes, so I can take some photographs?"

"Sure. Help yerself'," he said, lighting another cigarette. "I'm havin' a little bourbon and branch water. Care to join me?"

"No, thanks. Don't want to jeopardize my judgement," she said as she started snapping photographs.

Twenty minutes later she put her camera in its case, turned to Randy and said, "I'm finished. I have a very good idea of what's here. I'm ready to see what's in the shed."

They walked to a small building behind the shack, and he unlocked the door. Again, she stood in amazement at what was before her. Each wall of the shed had shelves that held Native American pieces. A stack of Native American rugs filled one corner. Bright headdresses and beaded work had been hung from nails in the walls. The shed was overflowing with incredibly beautiful pieces.

Marty's heart was racing, and her mouth felt dry as she looked at them.

I am so glad I didn't listen to Laura. This is one of the best days of my life. To have the opportunity to see these things is like I've been given a gift. I feel like I should pay him for allowing me to look at his collection.

She took more photos and after a half hour said, "All right, Mr. Jones. I'm ready to see what's in the cave."

As they walked over to the cave, he said, "First of all, name ain't Mr. Jones. It's Randy. Been Randy all my life, and I'm stayin' Randy. Second thing, think yer' gonna be surprised when you see the purties in my cave. Not many people have those things, specially since you can't buy 'em anymore, but that don't make no difference fer what yer' doin'."

"I'm sorry, but I don't understand what you mean."

"Jes' a minute and you'll unnerstan," he said. "Wait here." She watched as he pushed two large artificial boulders away from the entrance to the cave, opened a roughhewn wooden door, entered the cave, and lit several lanterns.

"Okay. Ya' can come in now."

She stepped into the cave and gasped.

CHAPTER THIRTEEN

Nothing in Marty Morgan's appraisal adventures had prepared her for this moment. Everywhere she looked were things she'd only read about. In the center of the cave, which extended back about fifty feet, was a huge piece of rock with pictographs of Native Americans doing a war dance.

Three walls of the cave were lined with shelves that held baskets, arrowheads, pottery, and just about every other type of Native American artifact there was. Her eyes swept the large cave for several moments, and then she turned to Randy, who was smiling broadly.

"So, whaddya think of my purties?" he asked.

"I've never seen anything like this. You have things here that aren't even in museums that specialize in Native American artifacts. I didn't think rock art could be bought."

"Can't. Had me a couple of suppliers over the years who knew where to go to get the good stuff. Lemme give ya' a 'lil tour. Course ya' can't tell people what I got in here. Might present some problems fer me if the law found out," he said, winking.

"I'll jes' tell ya' 'bout some of the rarer items. This here eagle feather headdress belonged to a chief. Don't think there's another one like it. And this Anasazi seed pot is in perfect condition, as ya' can see. I'm sure ya' know the Anasazi were Pre-Columbian so that puppy has a little age to it, like 'bout eight hunnert years or so. This here eagle claw necklace is the only one I've ever seen. Read me an article once that said one was found in Croatia that dated back over 130,000 years ago. Always been curious 'bout this one's age, but not curious enough to have some scientist turn it over to the Bureau of Land Management."

"Aren't you concerned about the legality of owning these items? Some of them sure look to me like they shouldn't be in a private collection."

"Nah," Randy said. "If'n no one knows about it, ain't illegal. Leastways that's how I look at it. Here's one of my favorites," he said lifting a mask off of a shelf. "It's a sacred Hopi Kachina mask. It's worth a bundle."

"Do you know where it came from?"

"Never asked. Imagine it might have spent some time at a burial ground, but makes no difference, cuz I'm the one who owns it now."

Marty shivered involuntarily. When she'd researched some of the Native American artifacts she'd done in past appraisals she remembered coming across an article about the illegal looting of burial grounds and people who sold the stolen items to collectors who didn't care where they came from. At the time she couldn't imagine anyone buying anything that had come from a burial ground. Now she was looking at someone who thought nothing of buying things that were illegal or from sacred burial grounds.

"If I were to keep one thing, might be this prayer stick with the eagle feathers. Guy I bought it from told me it was used in the Navajo Nation Holy Way ceremony. Don't know how they knew where somethin' like this was when they dug it up. It was used by the medicine men. Here's another thing them medicine men used. It's called a chamajillas or monster slayer stick. Comes from one of their bundles. Think maybe I mighta' been a medicine man in a past life. Anything that them medicine men used interests me."

Marty shook her head. "I don't know. I'm having a little problem with some of these things." She knew that a medicine man's bundle contained varied objects and representations of spiritual significance, from animal skins and effigies to ceremonial pipes and were passed from one keeper to another. It didn't seem right to have one in a non-Native American's collection of artifacts. She turned and looked at an item that was hanging from the net Randy had draped against one wall so he could display items. "That's a cradleboard isn't it?" she asked.

"Yeah," he said taking it off of the netting. "Remember when I was a kid in school and saw somethin' in a book 'bout Sacajawea carrying her kid in one when she was a guide fer Lewis and Clark. Always wanted one, but this one's special. Was tol' it was a board that probably belonged to the wife of a chief because of the eagle feathers and the beading on it. Don't know what that thing's worth. I've had it for a long time." He lit another cigarette and took a deep drag. "That's jes' some of the stuff. Take a little time and look around. Imagine you'll be wantin' to take some more pix, and then we can go back to the shack and talk about what yer' gonna charge me to do this, and when I can get it."

Forty-five minutes later Randy extinguished the lanterns and rolled the two pseudo-boulders back in front of the cave. They walked over to the shack. "So, whaddya think of my purties?" he asked.

"In all honesty, I don't know. I've never before seen many of the things you have. It's amazing."

"Yup. Figgered you'd say that. Now let's talk about dollars. That's what life's all about, right?"

"Not necessarily," Marty said.

"Well, whaddya think yer' gonna charge me fer writing up a report?"

"Look Randy, I might as well be honest with you. I'm really

concerned about some of the things you have in your collection. We both know they're illegal. If something is illegal and can't be bought or sold, how can I put a value on it?"

"Darlin', I got the buyers willin' to take that stuff. Ain't yer' problem. Now ya' jes' tell me what yer' report is gonna cost me."

"Let me sit down and do some calculations. I need to think about the research involved in this. It will probably take me three days to take the information and photographs of the collection, but the research is stumping me. I usually get in touch with museums and dealers to get comparables, but if something can only be bought and sold on the black market, I don't know how I'd go about that."

"Well, I'll save ya' the trouble. I know what I got, and I got a darned good idea of what it's worth. All I want from you is somethin' in writin' 'bout what the whole collection is worth. Shoot. I could probably do it in my sleep, but makes it more business-like if ya' put it on yer' official paper, if you know what I mean."

"Yes, I guess you're right. Here's my estimate," she said, handing him a piece of paper. "When would you like me to start?"

"As soon as possible. I'm kinda in a hurry to get this done. Got my reasons. Probably too late to start today," he said looking at his watch. "Anyway, I got some people comin' out here. How about say, eight tomorrow mornin'? I'm an early bird kinda person, and like I said, wanna get this over with."

"Fine," she said standing up. "That will give me time to do some preliminary research tonight. See you tomorrow morning. Do you want me to close the door?"

"Nah, leave it open. That breeze feels good. See ya' in the mornin'."

CHAPTER FOURTEEN

The killer turned his car onto the narrow dirt road that snaked its way along the floor of the canyon. He soon saw the old shack that was located on his right about two hundred feet up the side of a small ridge that rose from the edge of the road. There was an old orange truck parked in a turnout area next to the road that was large enough to hold two or three other vehicles. Next to the turnout was the start of a small foot path that led up the side of the ridge to the shack.

The killer opted not to park in the turnout, but instead drove several hundred yards past it and then turned off the road and parked behind several large boulders that concealed his car from view. He pulled on a pair of latex rubber gloves and picked up the tomahawk that was lying on the seat beside him. Using a towel he'd brought with him, he wiped down the tomahawk, removing any incriminating fingerprints that might have been on it. He quietly opened the car door and stepped out into the bright late afternoon sunshine. As he walked back to the dirt road, he tucked the tomahawk under his belt and pulled his shirt over it so it was concealed.

He easily made his way back to the turnout where the foot path was located and then started the short climb up the path that led to the shack. When he got to the top of the path he saw the shack that was built on a small level clearing in the side of the ridge. The door of the shack was wide open and was no more than twenty feet from where he was standing at the end of the foot path, and he could easily see into the shack. Randy Jones was sitting at a small table in the shack with his back to the open door, apparently looking at some papers that were on the table.

Okay, the killer thought, *it's now or never. I won't get a better opportunity than this. I'll be in and out in just a few minutes. He seems to be completely engrossed in looking at those papers, and he'll probably never even hear me when I sneak up behind him.*

The killer withdrew the tomahawk from his belt, crept up to the door of the shack, and stepped inside. Randy never knew what hit him as the killer smashed the tomahawk into the back of his head. Randy fell to the floor, obviously dead from the massive blow delivered by the tomahawk.

The killer glanced around the shack looking at the Native American artifacts that were everywhere in the small shack. Just as he was deciding what to do next, he heard the sound of a car door being slammed. He quickly moved to the door and peeked around the corner, making sure he wouldn't be seen. There was a car parked in the turnout, and he saw a woman standing next to it.

I don't know who this person is or why in the world she's out here in the middle of nowhere at this time of day, but I better get out of here pronto. I have no idea why anyone would want to come calling on Randy Jones, an old desert rat who currently is very, very dead and lying on the floor of his shack.

The killer darted out the door and made his way to the large boulders and rocks that surrounded the shack. Keeping the boulders between himself and the shack so he wouldn't be seen, he made his way down to the dirt road where he'd hidden his car. He started his car and turned left onto the narrow dirt road, knowing that the wind which had picked up would mask the sound of his car. Before he'd started today's little trip to pay a visit to Randy Jones, he'd checked the GPS map in his car, and he knew that by driving in the direction he was going, the narrow dirt road intersected a county gravel road only a mile or so ahead. The gravel road in turn intersected the main highway that connected High Desert and Palm Springs.

Once I'm on the main highway, I'll just blend in with the other traffic, and I'll be safe.

CHAPTER FIFTEEN

Marty drove away from Randy's shack feeling conflicted. On one hand the Native American collection was better than any she'd ever seen, and she was thrilled to have had the chance to see it in person, not just in books. On the other hand, she was well aware that a lot of the items, no, make it most of the items, had been purchased on the black market. Not only had the items been purchased on the black market, it was illegal to buy or sell them. Knowing that many of them had come from ancient tribal burial grounds spooked her.

If what Randy says is true, he's going to keep the appraisal, and the only thing he wants from me is a number, a number he can use so he can justify what he's going to ask for the collection. He mentioned two people who were interested in what he had. They must know it's illegal to buy or sell those items. Perhaps I could ask him to return the appraisal after he's shown them the value I place on the collection. Maybe that's what I should do.

She vacillated back and forth about whether it was ethical to do an appraisal of items that were going to be sold illegally based on her appraisal. Marty wondered whether or not it was a crime to do an appraisal of items that shouldn't be in a private collection, items that should be returned to their native tribe based on the Native American Graves Protection and Repatriation Act of 1990. She wondered if someone found out about it if she could be charged with being an accessory to a crime.

Ten minutes later, she made her mind up and turned the car around, making an illegal U-turn, and headed back to Randy's shack. *If I'm having this much inner conflict now, it's better for me to simply tell him I can't do the appraisal. I don't think I can live with myself if I do. The appraisal fee is not worth this much mental anguish. Nothing is worth what I'm feeling at the moment.*

She retraced her drive and parked her car in the same roadside turnout she'd used earlier. Marty opened her purse and took out her phone. She looked at it and realized she didn't have any signal strength bars which meant she couldn't call Jeff. Then she remembered when she and Randy had been walking over to the cave, he'd made an offhand comment that the only time he could get a cell phone connection was when he was standing next to the boulders in front of the cave. He told her he'd always thought that was an odd place for a connection.

Well, I'll call Jeff later and let him know I'm all right. When he comes to dinner tonight I can fill him in on the details.

Marty stepped out of her car, closed the door, slung her purse over her shoulder, took a deep breath and started walking up the footpath that led to the shack. As she was walking she mentally prepared herself to tell Randy she wasn't going to be able to do the appraisal. She was not looking forward to the next few minutes. What she didn't know was just how bad the next few minutes were going to be.

As she neared the door, she called out in a loud voice, "Randy, it's Marty. I'm back, and I want to talk to you for a minute." She saw that the door was still open, and she walked in. She took one look at Randy, who was lying on the floor with a tomahawk in the back of his head and screamed, running backwards to get away from the scene. For a moment she couldn't catch her breath or think what to do next, and then she remembered what Randy had said about the cell phone connection.

She stumbled several times as she hurried over to the boulders near the cave, and saw that there were bars displayed on her cell phone. She pressed in Jeff's number, and he answered on the first ring.

"Marty, is everything okay?" he asked.

"Nooo," she said trying to talk. "Jeff, he's dead. Randy's dead! Jeff, please come. I gave you the directions last night."

He interrupted her, "Take a deep breath. I'm on my way. Just answer one thing. Are you all right?"

"Yes, but Randy's de, dea, dead. He's got a tomahawk in the back of his head."

"Marty, stay away from him. Are you someplace where you can sit down?"

"Yes," she said sliding to the ground and putting her head between her knees. She knew from past experiences that if you felt like you were going to faint, it helped, and she definitely felt like she was going to faint.

"Marty, listen to me. I'll be there in about ten minutes. I'm calling the county sheriff. This is in his jurisdiction. I'm sure I'll be there before he is, but if he should get there before I do, it's okay. Just hang on. I'll drive as fast as I can. Do not go into the shack. Stay wherever you are. Will I be able to see you when I get there?"

"Yes," she sobbed. "I'm next to the two boulders that are in front of a cave."

"See you in a few minutes."

True to his word, Jeff came roaring up the narrow dirt road a few minutes later and came to a screeching halt in a cloud of dust. He flung the door of his car open and sprinted up the footpath. He spotted Marty slumped on the ground next to the cave entrance and rushed over to her. "Put your arm around my neck and let me help you stand up. The sheriff is on his way. Is Randy in the shack?"

"Yes," she said tearfully. "Oh, Jeff, I've never seen anything like that. Laura was right."

"I'm going over to the shack. Stay here. I'll be right back." He returned a few moments later and grimly said, "I've never seen anything like that either, and trust me, I've seen a lot in my thirty years as a cop."

CHAPTER SIXTEEN

Marty and Jeff heard the sirens approaching the shack, and moments later two sheriff's cars pulled to a stop on the dirt road below the shack. Three uniformed men quickly made their way up the trail. Jeff walked over to the first one and gestured towards the dilapidated shack. The officer motioned to the two men to follow him. In a few moments he stepped out of the shack and walked over to where Jeff was standing with Marty.

"I'm Sheriff Juan Antonio," he said to Marty. "I understand from Jeff you were the one who discovered the body. I'm sorry, but at some point, now or later, I'm going to need a statement from you." He turned to Jeff. "Coroner's on his way. From what I'm seeing in the shack, I think I better call the Bureau of Land Management, too. I'm sure they'll be very interested in some of those things he had in there."

Marty's eyelid was twitching furiously, and Jeff knew by the telltale sign she was even more nervous than she was letting on. "Marty, can you tell us what happened? I thought you were going to be up here earlier this afternoon. I've been waiting for your call."

She started to talk but was interrupted by the sheriff. "Do you mind if I record this? I can use it as your statement, and you won't have to tell it again."

"Sure, that's fine." For the next half hour Marty told them everything that had happened from the time she'd first gotten to the shack to when she'd returned, including what Randy had shown her in the shed and the cave.

"Marty, did you see anything suspicious while you were with Randy? Did you notice anything that would make you think someone was lurking nearby?" Jeff asked

"No, nothing, but then again, I was so caught up in the unbelievable collection of artifacts I was seeing, I'm not sure it would have even registered."

A few minutes later a dark government looking sedan pulled to a stop on the road below, and a man waved to Jeff and Juan when he got out of it. He walked up the path and Juan introduced him, "Marty, this is Rich Willis with the BLM. Rich, Marty Morgan. She's an appraiser Randy was going to hire to appraise his Native American collection. Looks like he had a lot of things he shouldn't have had."

"Marty, I'm sorry to ask you this," Rich said, "because I'm sure this has been a horrible experience for you, but would you mind telling me what Randy said about his collection? If you're not up to it, I won't ask you to go back in the shack, but would you mind walking through the shed and the cave with me? Again, I'm sorry to ask you this, but I'm concerned that as soon as the word gets out that Randy's dead, people who know about his collection will try to loot it."

"Did you know him?" Marty asked.

"Not personally. I'm not at liberty to say much at this point, but let's say Randy Jones and his collection have been of interest to the Bureau of Land Management for a long time. There's a man in our department who's an undercover agent who has a pretty good idea what Randy had out here, but I'd like to hear your side of it."

"Rich, I just thought of something. When I was going through the shack, the shed, and the cave, I took a lot of photographs. I can send them to you and you could send them to the undercover agent. Maybe they'll be of some help. Actually, I'd like to think that something good will come from this day."

"That would be great. Here's my email address," he said writing it on the back of his business card. "You can upload them to your computer and send them to me. I'll see that he gets them. Are you sure you're all right with going back in these places?"

"Yes. I'll be fine." She turned to Jeff. "How long do you think he'd been dead when you saw him?"

"Not long. Not long at all. I'm just glad it wasn't you. I wonder who would want to kill Randy and why. His next of kin needs to be notified."

"I don't think that will be necessary. He told me the only next of kin he had was a son he hadn't seen in over forty years and didn't know where he was."

"Well," the sheriff said. "We'll start looking into it. With a collection like he had, his death might very well have been about it. Hate to put you on the spot, Marty, but can you ball park what his collection would be worth?"

"As I explained earlier, how can you put a value on something that's illegal to buy or sell?"

"I know what you're saying, but look at it this way. It's illegal to buy or sell cocaine, but there's still a price put on it."

"Good point. I'm going to say a figure that keeps popping up in front of my eyes. Five million."

The sheriff whistled. "Wow! That alone would be a motive for murder. I suppose the good thing is that no one can say that your valuation is wrong."

For the first time she laughed. "All right, gentlemen. I'll give you the tour and tell you what Randy told me about the items. Let me get my notes, and I'll be right back with you."

The sheriff, Rich, and Jeff listened as she described the items in the shed and cave. At the end of an hour she said, "That's pretty much it. I really am tired. Would it be all right if I leave now?"

"Yes, and we really thank you. I've recorded everything, and I'll get it to my undercover man. He's probably going to want to talk to you. Would it be all right with you if I gave him your contact information?"

"Absolutely. I'd be happy to help in any way, if I can. Actually, I'd like to find out who did this. Randy was definitely a character, but no one deserves to die the way he did."

CHAPTER SEVENTEEN

Marty followed Jeff back to the compound in her car after assuring him she was calm enough to drive. As usual, Duke was at the gate watching for her. They each got out of their cars and started to walk up to the gate. Jeff put his hand on the gate, stopping her, and said, "I hope you don't mind, but I called John and told him what happened today. I didn't want you to have to relive it one more time by telling everyone. You've been through enough today. John said to tell you he'd made a big batch of gazpacho for the food truck earlier and had enough left over for dinner tonight. He also said he'd make some soft fish tacos to go with it. He was going to tell Laura and Les, so you don't have to, but I imagine all of them will be worried about you."

"Thanks. I'm glad you called him. I know Laura would never say she told me so, but if I were her I'd be thinking that. At the moment I could use a glass of wine and a quick shower. I not only feel the desert dust and dirt on me with the way that wind was blowing today, but I'd also like to try and wash away what I saw today."

"As someone who's had to view more than a few scenes like that, I wish I could tell you a shower will help get rid of it. Problem is, it doesn't. It may wash the desert grime off, but the memory of what you saw will still be there. What I will tell you is that time's a wonderful healer. I'll personally make sure you have some good memories to cover the bad ones. Fair enough?" he asked, grinning.

"Very fair, and believe me, I'm ready for some better memories other than what I have of today."

As soon as they walked through the gate and greeted Duke, Laura walked over to Marty and hugged her. "I'm so sorry you had to be the one to find the man who was murdered. It must have been horrible."

Marty stepped back and looked at her. "You knew something like that was going to happen, didn't you? That's why you didn't want me to take that appraisal."

"My extra sensory powers aren't usually quite that specific. I kept getting the feeling you were in danger, and I was very concerned. I was so concerned I called Jeff and asked him to stay somewhere close to where you were. I told him I was sure you were going to call him, and you'd need him."

Marty looked at Jeff. "You didn't tell me that was why you stayed nearby."

He looked abashed and said, "I wasn't going to say anything, but your sister was pretty adamant that I be on standby. I'd told you I wouldn't be down in Palm Springs, but actually, I spent a lot of time at the Hi-Lo talking to Lucy. She's quite a character. Did you know she has a photographic memory when it comes to certain things?"

"No. She's never mentioned it. Like what things?"

"She told me she never forgets a license plate number or who buys what kind of cigarettes from her at the drugstore. She said it's really annoying, because once she sees a license plate or sells someone cigarettes, it's in her memory bank." He laughed. "She went on to say that she probably should work someplace where there weren't so many cars going in and out of the parking lot and people buying cigarettes, because her mind goes on overload."

"What a strange type of mental ability to possess. I'm sure there's some way she could make that work for her, but at the moment it's not coming to me. I'll be back in a few minutes. I really do need to shower. Come on, Duke," she said as she walked into her house.

Jeff and Laura walked over to the long picnic table in the courtyard and sat down. Les came out of his house carrying a bottle of wine. "Jeff, I heard you drive up and figured you could use a glass of wine. The glasses are already on the table."

"Jeff, how's Marty doing? She looks pretty pale," Laura said.

"It's never easy seeing an individual who has just been murdered, particularly when it involves a tomahawk. I'm sure it will take her a little time to get over this. What's really sad is if she hadn't been so conscientious about her appraisals, she wouldn't have been the one to find Randy."

"What do you mean? I have to tell you I had a premonition that some of the things she was going to see were very dark, as if there were spirits associated with them."

"You were right. Marty initially left his shack to come home, but then she decided she couldn't ethically do the appraisal because so many of the items in the collection were obviously stolen from sacred Native American burial grounds. She went back to tell Randy, and that's when she discovered his body."

"How horrible, but I have to say I admire her for doing it. I hope she doesn't get any ideas about trying to find out who murdered him. She helped solve the Jensen case, but that was probably a fluke. You might want to mention that to her. I don't think she'll take it from me at the moment," Laura said.

"I will."

Just then John, the portly owner of The Red Pony food truck, walked out of the fourth house that formed a compound around the courtyard. "Jeff, I'm glad you were able to help Marty. Sounds like she had a really bad afternoon. Max is in the kitchen making the salsa for the fish tacos, and I have some killer gazpacho. I hope that will help. I'm a firm believer that good food makes everything seem better."

"I couldn't agree more. Sure is in my case, but everyone, please let's all be a little gentle with Marty for the next couple of days. She's been through a lot, and it's going to take some time for her to get through this," Jeff said. "Believe me, I speak from experience."

The door to Marty's house opened, and she and Duke walked out and came over to the table. "Before anyone says anything, because I don't want to start crying, I just want you to know how glad I am that all of you are here. I'm with my best friends, and that gives me a good feeling after the terrible events of today."

"Does that mean I've been demoted from a possible romantic future to one of friendship," Jeff asked in a joking manner.

Laura noticed he was rubbing his index finger and thumb together. She knew from being with him in the past that was his tell, or in psychic speak, she knew he was nervous.

Interesting. He comes off as an all polished I'm in control Mr. Detective, but underneath there's a little boy who's afraid of being rejected. I sure hope Marty sees that and doesn't hurt him.

"No, Jeff, you haven't been demoted. I've had people tell me that their best friend was their husband."

"Does that mean you're proposing to me?" he asked.

"Possibly. After today, I may need someone to take care of me."

"This is a subject that definitely needs to be pursued at a later…"

Jeff was interrupted by a call from Max, asking John to come into the kitchen and help him serve the gazpacho. A few moments later bowls of chilled gazpacho garnished with chives had been put in front of everyone.

"Dig in," John said. "I pay Max enough that he can take care of barbecuing the fish while I eat with you, which is something I don't get to do very often."

As usual, whatever John served was excellent, and the gazpacho was no exception. Laura was the first to speak. "John, I've never had your gazpacho before, and it's definitely the best I've ever had."

"Thanks. I serve it a lot at The Red Pony because I can make a big batch of it a day or so ahead of time. It keeps beautifully. I don't serve bowls this big at The Pony. I serve it in little paper cups. People usually buy it in place of a salad and have it along with a sandwich. It's kind of a Southwest thing, plus it's pretty. I'd offer you seconds, but I don't want you to be so full you won't eat one of my fish tacos."

He stood up and walked into his kitchen returning with a large tray which held warm tortillas, homemade fresh salsa, and cabbage tossed with a bit of ranch dressing and lime juice. He deftly cut the fish into pieces and said, "Please, help yourselves."

"John, I've had a lot of fish tacos over the years, but I've never had one that was this simple and tasted this fresh. Usually the fish is fried with a heavy batter and piled with all kinds of things that really don't taste that good. Is this something you serve at The Pony?"

"I can answer that, Les," Max, John's assistant said. "On the days when we serve it, maybe once a week, I set up a barbecue next to the truck to cook the fish, and we always sell out. Right, John?"

"Yes. It really is one of our best sellers. Since we're all stuffed, I'm going to bring out a little treat to sweeten your mouth. A customer brought me one of these a few days ago, and it was so good I asked her for the recipe. Back in a minute." He returned with a plate of what looked like chocolate covered pretzels.

"John, these look wild! What are they?" Marty asked.

"Exactly what they look like. A chocolate covered pretzel with a pecan in the middle. It's a very interesting combination of flavors, sweet, salty, and nutty. I think I need to put these on the menu."

Jeff spoke up. "Everyone, this has been a great way to end a horrible day, but if anyone's noticed, Marty's eyes are starting to get glassy looking, and she can barely keep them open. Think it's time for her to go to bed. I'm going to tuck her in and give her a couple of aspirin so she can sleep. As always, thanks, John." He stood up and walked around the table to Marty. "Come on, sleepy. Time for bed."

Jeff walked Marty into her house and told her to get ready for bed. "Duke, hate to do the bootie bit, but tonight Marty's really tired, so I'm the one who will have to take you for your evening walk. Thank heavens we're far out here in the desert, and it's dark. Don't want anyone to see me doing this. Come on, boy, let's get these things on." He struggled with the booties and after a few minutes took Duke out to commune with nature and the desert floor.

When they walked back into Marty's house, she was already asleep. Duke settled in on his bed and looked balefully at Jeff as he kissed Marty on the forehead. He found a bottle of aspirin in the bathroom and put it on her nightstand along with a note on which he'd written "You know you can call me anytime if you want to talk." He leaned down and whispered, "Good night, sweetheart. I promise tomorrow will be a better day."

CHAPTER EIGHTEEN

Although Marty had easily gone to sleep, the night was not kind to her. She woke up several times feeling like she was suffocating. Finally dawn came, and she wearily got out of bed and made a pot of coffee. She had the feeling she'd overlooked something from the prior day's events. The more she thought about it, the more certain she was that the killer had been on Randy's property when she'd gone back to talk to him. She wracked her brain, but nothing came to her. At 7:30 her phone rang.

"Good morning, sunshine. I hope you had a good night's sleep," Jeff said.

"Well, I can lie or be truthful. Which do you want?"

"Might as well go for the truth. By that I take it you didn't sleep well."

She sighed. "Jeff, I feel certain I'm overlooking something. The killer must have still been on Randy's property when I went back there. Both you and the sheriff said he'd only been dead for a few minutes. I probably interrupted him. It gives me the willies to think he may have seen me. Do you think he did?" she asked, grimacing at the thought.

Jeff was quiet. "If it's any consolation, I didn't sleep well either.

Yes, that thought also occurred to me. Did you see any cars when you went back?"

"No, and if someone was there, they had to drive out to Randy's place. It's too remote for someone to just walk up to it. For the life of me, I can't figure out what it is that I'm missing."

"Maybe it's just your imagination. I wish I could be with you today, but I have to go to work. There's a case that needs my attention, and I don't think the captain would be very happy if I told him a woman I care a great deal about was more important than my job."

She was quiet for a moment, knowing that they were getting close to the time when decisions needed to be made about their relationship. The events of yesterday, and Jeff's concern for her left no doubt about his intentions. She didn't know if that included marriage, but it certainly wasn't out of the realm of possibility. If anyone had told her when she was leaving the Midwest that she would seriously consider getting married again, she would have said they were crazy. It wasn't sounding so crazy anymore.

"Thank you, Jeff, and thanks for being there for me yesterday. Do what you need to do today. I assume you're coming to dinner tonight. I think John would be devastated if you weren't here, but I'm beginning to think I would be too. John told me last night that it wasn't half as much fun when you and I weren't there. He wished you'd come to dinner while I was in Chicago."

"I'll remember that the next time you go out of town, and since I don't want to disappoint your pal John, tell him I'll be there for sure. What's on your schedule today?"

"I think I'll take some time off for a couple of days. Laura mentioned that the insurance company wanted me to do an appraisal for the desert home of the man whose Tiffany collection I did in Chicago. I may just veg until then."

"Sounds like a good idea. I'll see you tonight. Take care of yourself."

Marty got dressed, bootied up Duke, and took him outside. Something was still nagging her, something she'd missed yesterday. She couldn't put the thought out of her mind. It was like it was on a loop and kept repeating itself, over and over.

Although I hate to ask her, I wonder if Laura has any ideas about what it is I'm missing. With her psychic ability, she might come up with something. I'm sure she's up and getting ready for work.

She knocked on Laura's door which was opened a moment later. "Marty, how are you doing?" she asked as she motioned for Marty and Duke to come in. "I spent all night thinking about you."

"That's why I'm here. Is there anything you can tell me about what happened yesterday? I'm really frustrated, because I feel like I'm missing something."

"I think you are. I'm not exactly sure what it is, but I've had the same feeling. It has something to do with a clue to the murder, and I'm pretty sure it's out on Randy's property. Problem is, I knew if I told you you'd want to go out there, and given everything that's happened I'm not sure that's a good idea. I'm sure Jeff wouldn't think it was a good idea. I watched him last night, and he did that thing where he rubs his thumb and his index finger together whenever he's nervous. I think he's very nervous about you."

Marty smiled. "I like him a lot more than I realized. After I found out that Scott was having an affair with his secretary and wanted out of our twenty-five year marriage, I swore off men. I can't believe I'm letting one into my life and thinking of letting him in permanently."

Laura gave her a hug. "I think you could do a lot worse. He's a good man, and he seems to have your best interests at heart. A lot of relationships have started with less."

"I just thought of something, Laura. The county sheriff and the man from the Bureau of Land Management decided to station a guard on Randy's property until they could get a court order to remove the items from the scene of the crime. They were afraid of looting once word got out that Randy was dead. A lot of people knew he had some very good Native American artifacts. Tell you what. I'm going out to Randy's property and see what I can come up with, but only if the guard is there. I'll identify myself, but I promise if there isn't a guard, I won't stay. Does that sound okay to you? After all, you're the one who knows stuff," she said, grinning at her sister.

"If you can promise me that, I won't feel like I have to call Jeff and tell him. Yes, that sounds okay. I'm not getting any bad feelings about it. I have to go to work now, but tonight I definitely want to hear what, if anything, you find out, and I have a feeling you'll find something. I also have a feeling you're not going to be too sure what to do with it. I'm getting vibes that you need to talk to a Native American woman."

"What do you mean by that?"

"I have no idea. That's just the feeling I'm getting. See you later."

Duke and Marty walked the few steps back to her house. "Time for breakfast, Duke. Come." Later she heard John leave in The Red Pony, and she thought once again how lucky she was to be living in a place that had its own resident chef.

CHAPTER NINETEEN

"Duke, I'm whipped, and that bed of mine looks awfully inviting. I'm going to see if I can get a little sleep. If I went out to Randy's as tired as I am right now, I'm sure I'd miss whatever it is I'm supposed to see." She lay down on her bed and within minutes was asleep.

Marty woke with a start, trying to figure out what time of day or night it was. She vaguely remembered lying down, but she had no idea how long she'd been asleep. She looked over at the clock on the nightstand.

Well, that's a first, she thought. *I've been asleep for five hours. It's already two in the afternoon.*

Within minutes she'd showered and dressed. "Come on Duke, time to go outside. I need to go out to Randy's and figure out what I've missed. I'm sorry you can't come with me, but I have no idea how long I'll be there, and I don't want to leave you in the car."

Marty told him to stay as she opened the compound gate and walked to her car. She thought about taking her camera, but decided if she did need to take a photograph, she could use her cell phone.

When she got to the parking area near Randy's shack, she noticed a sheriff's car. *Good,* she thought, *that means they must have posted a guard, and it's safe for me to go up there.* The only other vehicle she saw was

Randy's old orange truck.

She walked up the footpath to where Randy's shack was located and saw that yellow tape had been placed across the entrances to the shack, the shed, and the cave. A man in a sheriff's uniform was sitting in a chair outside the shack reading a magazine. He looked up as she walked towards him, hand near the gun he wore on his hip.

"Hello, I'm Marty Morgan," she said walking up to him. "I'm the appraiser who discovered Randy's body yesterday. I had a long talk with Sheriff Antonio and the man from the BLM, Rich Willis. They told me they were going to post a guard. I assume that must be why you're here. Right?"

The deputy sheriff stood up and shook her hand while he said, "My name is Sam Loomis. That must have been quite a sight. Don't think I've ever heard of a murder that involved a tomahawk. I'm surprised you're back here."

"For some reason, I have this feeling that I missed something yesterday. Would it be all right with you if I spent a little time just looking around? I don't even know what I'm looking for."

"Sure. Help yourself, but if you do find something that could be used as evidence, you'll have to leave it with me."

"Of course. Thank you."

She looked at the shack, the shed, and the cave, not quite sure where to begin. While she was standing there deciding what to do next, she suddenly realized what it was she'd overlooked yesterday. "I think I'll start here and work my way over to the shed and cave. It shouldn't take me very long." She knew exactly where she needed to go, but she didn't want the deputy to accompany her.

Marty walked around the shack several times, looking at the walls and the ground, then did the same with the shed. The deputy sheriff became engrossed in the magazine he'd been reading when she first saw him. While he was reading it she walked over to the where the cave was located.

When I called Jeff yesterday after I'd discovered Randy's body, I had to walk over here to get cell phone reception, and although it didn't register at the time, I vaguely remember seeing some cigarette butts that didn't look like the kind Randy smoked, but I don't remember exactly where I was standing.

She took her phone out of her purse and walked past the entrance of the cave and the two artificial boulders next to it until she saw the signal connection bars pop up on her cell phone. *This must be where I stood. I was so shaken by seeing Randy I simply forgot exactly where I was standing.*

Marty looked down at the desert ground and spotted three cigarette butts. She looked back at the deputy who was still engrossed in his magazine.

She quickly took several photos of the exact location of the cigarette butts with her phone and slipped it back into her purse. Marty knelt down and picked the cigarettes up with the Kleenex she'd taken out of her purse. *Maybe I can get Jeff to run a fingerprint test for me. I'm sure they're not Randy's. I definitely remember he smoked nonfiltered cigarettes, and these have a filter.* She put them in the side pocket of her purse and spent a few more minutes walking around as if she was still looking for something.

Several minutes later she walked over to Deputy Loomis and said, "Well, I was hoping I could find something, but I didn't. Obviously the feeling I had was wrong. I was so shaken up when I saw Randy I was afraid I'd missed something. Looks like I didn't. Thanks for letting me walk around. How long are guards going to be posted out here?"

"I don't know. It depends on whether or not the sheriff can get a judge to sign an order allowing the sheriff's department and the BLM to remove all of the artifacts. I hear Randy didn't have any next of kin, and from what I was told, looks like a lot of this stuff should be returned to the tribes they belong to. I know that dealing in stuff like that is a billion dollar a year business, but it gives me the creeps.

You'd never catch me digging up someone's grave. Hope they find out who killed Randy and hope they find out who took the stuff from the Indians in the first place, but I'm sure that's probably not going to happen."

"Unfortunately, I imagine you're right, but I guess maybe if these things are returned to their rightful owners, some justice will be done."

"Nice meeting you, Ms. Morgan. Probably won't see you again and sorry you had to be the one to discover him. Things like that can stay with you for a while."

"Yes. I've heard it's just going to take some time. So long."

She walked back down the path, got in her car, and began to drive down the road. As soon as she saw bars on her cell phone, she pulled off the road and called Jeff. "Jeff, I'm sorry to bother you at work, but could I come to your office? I need to show you something."

"Marty, is everything all right? You sound pretty excited."

"I am, and I think you will be too. Is it okay if I come over now? I can't wait until I see you tonight."

"Those are the words every man wants to hear. How long will it take for you to get here?"

"I should be there in about half an hour. Can you take a coffee break? I could meet you at that coffee shop next to the station."

"Sure. I'll meet you there in half an hour. You may be excited, but promise me you'll drive safely."

"I will. See you in a little while."

CHAPTER TWENTY

Marty parked in the last available spot in the coffee shop parking lot and walked in the door. She spotted Jeff sitting at a booth facing the door with two cups of coffee already on the table. She hurried over to him and gave him a kiss on the cheek.

"Well, that's a nice way to begin the late afternoon. What did I ever do to deserve that?"

"Just trying to keep your downtown image intact. I imagine you have women walk up to you all the time giving you a kiss," she said as she laughed and sat down.

"Fraid not sweetheart, but any time you want to repeat that, you have my permission."

"Jeff, I'm pretty excited. I was able to find a couple of clues, and I need your help." She told him about going to Randy's, and what she'd found.

"Marty, I really wish you hadn't gone out there. I would have been happy to go with you. I'm glad it worked out, but that's the kind of thing you do that drives me nuts. I'm a detective. I'm supposed to protect and help people. I'm supposed to solve crimes. What I'm not supposed to do is spend all my time worrying about you. Oh well, I can see that it's hopeless," he said in a slightly raised voice. "You are what you are. Let's see what you've got."

She took the Kleenex with the cigarette butts out of the side pocket of her purse and showed them to him. He spent a few moments looking at them and then said, "I saw the coroner's report this morning. Did you know that Randy had lung cancer? These must have been his."

"Randy had lung cancer? He didn't tell me that, although I bet that's the reason he wanted to sell his collection. He probably knew he was going to die. Wow!" She sat back in the booth and took a sip of her coffee. "Jeff, these aren't his. The whole time I was with Randy he smoked one cigarette after another, and they definitely weren't filtered cigarettes. These are filtered cigarettes, and they can't be his."

"Are you sure he didn't smoke Desert Springs?"

"Is that their name? How do you know?"

"I had a partner who was a chain smoker, and that was his brand. There was always an ashtray full of them on his desk. It was when you could still smoke in the workplace. Glad it's illegal to smoke in an office now. Anyway, those are definitely Desert Springs cigarette butts."

"Jeff, I think they're from the killer. I found them slightly behind the boulder to the right of the cave entrance. Someone could hide behind the boulder, and by peeking around it, have a straight view into Randy's house. Remember, he left the door open for the breeze. Maybe he was even there before I left the first time and was waiting for me to leave. Anyway, can you run a fingerprint test on them?"

"That would be a little tricky, Marty. First of all, you need to turn these over to the sheriff. There's a good possibility they have something to do with the murder, and the case falls under his jurisdiction. Secondly, I'm not working on any cases at the moment that involve cigarettes. It would sure make everybody suspicious if I suddenly asked the lab to run some tests on these cigarette butts. I don't see how I could do it, and even if I could think of a way to do it, if anyone ever found out that I, sworn to uphold the law, did something like this, I could be fired."

Marty's face fell. "Jeff, you know I'd never do anything to jeopardize your job, but isn't there some way we can find out if fingerprints on these butts match someone's fingerprints? If nothing shows up, I can turn them over to the sheriff and say that I put them in the pocket of my purse when I was calling you after I'd seen Randy, but I was so distraught, I completely forget about it."

"What do you intend to do if there is a match?" he asked.

She held the coffee cup up to her lips. "I don't know, but it would be a start. I guess it would depend on who it was."

"In order for there to be a match a person must have their fingerprints in the system. If they aren't in the system, in other words if they've never been fingerprinted, we'll never know whose fingerprints are on these butts. Anyway, it's a non-issue, because I can't just take them to the lab and tell them I need it for a case I'm working on. I would have to get the chief's signature on something like that, and there's no way he's going to do it."

Marty started to wrap the Kleenex around the butts when Jeff put his hand over hers. "All right. I can't stand to see you looking so sad. I'll take them. Actually I've done a couple of favors for the head of the fingerprinting department. It involved his son and drugs. He's indebted to me. Let me see what I can come up with. I'll give him a call right now."

He took his cell phone out of his shirt pocket and pressed in a number. "Hi, Lou, it's Jeff Combs." He listened for a minute. "I'm fine. How's your son doing these days?" Again he listened. "Glad to hear that. Looks like we can put that whole incident to bed, and I'm sure that's a chapter in your life you'd like to forget. I have a favor to ask of you. Actually, it's a huge favor. I have some cigarette butts in my possession, and I'd like you to run a fingerprint test on them and see if you can get a match. This is on the QT. Nothing illegal, just rather no one in my department knew about it."

Marty heard Lou say that would be fine and asked Jeff if he could come to his office right away. He told Jeff that one of his employees had called in sick that morning and the other one had arranged to take the afternoon off some time ago. There was no one in the office but him for the rest of the afternoon, so it would be a perfect time for him to privately run some tests.

Jeff stood up and said, "I'm on my way, Lou. Be there in five minutes. Thank you so much." He turned to Marty. "That was a serendipitous stroke of luck." He carefully wrapped the Kleenex around the butts and put them into a baggie he always carried with him. He'd learned long ago to keep one, just in case. This was definitely a "just in case."

"Go. I'll leave a tip and see you tonight. How long do you think it will take? Will you know anything tonight?" she asked.

"I should. See you later."

CHAPTER TWENTY-ONE

After Marty walked out of the coffee shop, she decided to stop by Carl Mitchell's antique shop on the way home. Even though she wasn't going to do the appraisal of Randy's collection, she knew Carl could probably help her find the names of the two people Randy had mentioned were going to visit him later on the afternoon of his death, the doctor and the dealer.

"Marty, how good to see you. It's been awhile," Carl said when she opened the door to the Palm Springs Antique Shoppe. "Actually other than waving to you at a couple of our appraiser events, I don't think we've had a chance to talk since your sister used the butcher knife on the styrofoam wig stand head, and the diamond ring popped out."

"I know that kind of freaked you out, Carl, and I'm sorry, but there's some saying like 'all's well that ends well.' Actually think it's from a play by Shakespeare, but it seems appropriate here. I'm sure you heard that Pam's murderer was caught and is in jail waiting for his trial. I understand he's still refusing to accept a plea bargain even though his attorney has been pushing it for weeks."

"I've heard that, too. Coincidentally, I had dinner the other night at Mai Tai Mama's, and it was delicious. I understand Pam's son is running it now and doing a darned good job."

"I've heard the same. Let me change the subject. Have you ever heard of a man named Randy Jones? He collected Native American artifacts."

"Yes. He came in here from time to time to see if I had any Native American artifacts. He never bought anything of mine, and I heard this morning that he was murdered yesterday. Evidently the killer used a tomahawk. Why do you ask?"

"I was the one who found him. It's a long story, and not a very pretty one. I'm trying to get rid of the memory, and I'm not having very much luck. Anyway, when I was with him earlier in the day he mentioned that two people were going to come to his house, or rather shack, that afternoon. He was going to offer to sell his collection to them. One was a dealer, probably engages in some black market activity from what I saw, and the other one was a prominent doctor. Either one of those people ring a bell with you?"

"Marty, there are a lot of people in the desert who own and collect Native American artifacts. Let me think for a minute." He stood lost in thought and then walked into a back room that Marty presumed was his office. A few minutes later he returned with a business card in his hand.

"A man came in here several months ago and asked if I had any Anasazi pottery in very good condition or top-notch Cahuilla baskets. I told him I didn't really deal in Native American artifacts, but from time to time I'd hear about somebody who wanted to sell pieces. He gave me his card and asked me to call him if I ever heard of someone who was interested in selling the types of pieces he collected. I don't remember much about him, other than he was very intense."

"Would you mind if I took down that information? Maybe he's the one who was going to go out to Randy's, although I can't imagine what connection they would have."

"Collecting makes strange bedfellow, believe me. You can take the card, Marty, but I have to ask why you want it. I hope you're not thinking of trying to find the killer. Didn't you get enough of danger and crime on that Jensen appraisal you did, the one where you were almost killed?"

She sighed. "Carl, Randy was an eccentric man who probably did a lot of things in the collecting arena I'd rather not know about, but I was the last person to see him alive other than his murderer. I feel like I have a responsibility to see what I can find out. After all, he did call me to do the appraisal. I keep thinking if I'd gone back to his shack a few minutes earlier, or if I'd begun the appraisal while I was originally there, Randy would still be alive. I can't put that thought out of my mind. If there's anything I can do to help solve this crime and have the person who's responsible for his murder caught, I will."

"I can understand that. I've heard you're seeing Detective Combs. How does he feel about this? I imagine he'd rather let the experts do their job instead of you becoming involved."

"That's a pretty good assessment of the situation, but I'm already involved in this, so I might as well do whatever I can to help."

"Okay. As far as the name of the dealer, you might want to talk to Colin Sanders. I don't have any way to get in touch with him, but you could probably find him on the Internet. He's got a reputation for having some very good artifacts, but he also has a reputation for acquiring pieces that aren't legal to buy or sell. Of course that doesn't seem to matter much when it comes to collecting Native American artifacts. If a collector is willing to pay the price, someone else is willing to get whatever it is they need, even if it's not done legally. Marty, be careful. You're getting into some murky waters that might be better left to professionals rather than an attractive middle-aged woman."

"I appreciate your concern and thanks for the names. I better get back to the compound. Time to feed and water my dog. I've left him alone long enough." She gave Carl a cheery wave as she walked out.

If I'm not at the compound when Jeff gets there, he'll worry, and then so will everybody else. I have enough on my mind without making the situation any worse than it is.

She got in her car and began the half hour drive to the High Desert compound where she lived.

CHAPTER TWENTY-TWO

As soon as Marty returned to the compound, she bootied up Duke and took him for a walk, feeling a little guilty about having left him alone for so long. "Sorry, big guy, I really wasn't expecting to be gone that long. Les is always so good about walking you when I'm gone, that I promise I'll let him know so this doesn't happen again."

After the walk, she fed him and then went out to the courtyard. Laura waved as she walked in her house. "Give me a minute. I need to change clothes."

Les, John, and Max were already sitting at the courtyard table. "Hi, guys. How went the painting and the food truck today?" she asked the resident artist and the two food truck men.

"Working on a piece I really like. Think it will probably be exhibited at the show I'm having at the Moore Gallery in a few months."

"The food truck business is huge," John said. "It seems to be growing by the day. One of the best decisions I ever made was to quit my job working at Smokey's Restaurant and start up The Red Pony. What's also amazing is that I'm developing quite a catering business. I wasn't expecting that. If it keeps up, I might have to rent a commercial kitchen in the Springs and hire a couple more people. Max and I are having a hard time keeping up with the demand."

"Sounds kind of like a double-edged sword. On one hand business is good, but on the other hand you can't keep up with the demand," Marty said. "I'd bet a lot of people would love to have that problem. From what you're telling me, if you don't rent a kitchen, there's a very good chance you won't be able to continue your level of excellence in both the catering and at the food truck. Sound about right?"

"Unfortunately, I think you just nailed it. Believe me, I'm struggling with it. I'm going to have the best year financially I've ever had, but I'm beginning to think I'm going to pay a high price for it. Take tonight, for example. You know how much I love trying out new recipes on my compound mates, but I'm so tired the only thing I could think to have that wouldn't require much work is some bread, cheese, and deli meats, and those are all leftover from the truck."

"You don't have to apologize for that meal," Les said. "It's always been one of my favorite things. Think I was a cow in a past life, because I love to graze, a little of this, a little of that. Sounds wonderful."

"Thanks, that makes me feel better. I appreciate the money you all give me each month in return for me fixing dinner and using you as guinea pigs, but I'm not sure I'm worth it about now," John said in a small voice. "Oh, there is one good thing. I made a couple of carrot cakes early this morning, and even though they're delicious, they didn't sell out, so at least you'll have something homemade tonight."

"I absolutely love carrot cake," Marty said. "When we were kids, mom used to make it for us. Laura likes it as much as I do. You won't get any complaints from us."

"Again, thanks."

Laura's door opened and she walked out and joined them in the warm fall evening. "I thought I heard something about carrot cake. Please tell me it wasn't a figment of my imagination," she said as she sat down and put her hand affectionately on Les' hand.

"Truth be told, it's carrot cake for dessert, but first I want to sit here and relax for a while. Looks like Jeff's here. I see his car pulling up in front of the compound."

Marty felt her heart begin to speed up, and Laura looked at her curiously. *How in the devil can she know I'm nervous about what he found out? Oh, yeah, there goes my eyelid. I can't ever have a case of the nervies without everyone knowing about it. Guess I'm too old to outgrow it.*

She stood up and greeted Jeff as he walked over to the table. He whispered, "No news yet. I'm expecting a phone call. Be patient."

The two of them sat down at the table and soon they were sharing the details of their day. Marty didn't say much. She wasn't sure she wanted Jeff to know she planned on following up on the information Carl had given her. Although Jeff hadn't told her not to try and find out who murdered Randy, instinctively she knew he wouldn't be happy about what she planned to do.

John and Max excused themselves and returned shortly with a platter containing an arrangement of baguettes, several kinds of cheese, sliced turkey, and ham. "As I said guys, I'm tired, so instead of nicely putting all of the condiments in little dishes with spoons, tonight we're using the things exactly as they came out of the pantry or the refrigerator."

They were just finishing dinner when Jeff excused himself. "Sorry, this is a call I have to take. I'll be back in a few minutes." He walked to the gate and listened to what the person on the other end was saying, and then Marty could see him talking. He ended the call, and as he walked back to the table, he looked at Marty and moved his head imperceptibly from side to side, indicating no.

"Jeff, you don't look very happy. Something wrong?" Laura asked.

He turned to Marty, "Do you mind if I tell them what you found today?"

"No," she said in a sad voice.

Jeff explained what Marty had found, and how he'd called in an old favor from a friend who worked at the crime lab. His friend had just told him that there was no match to the fingerprints found on the discarded cigarette butts Marty had found. Jeff went on to tell the others that while he wasn't very happy about Marty's involvement in the case, he understood why she was interested in finding out who murdered Randy. After all, she very easily could have been a target herself.

"Marty, do you think the killer saw you? Or knows who you are?" Laura asked.

"I have no idea. I didn't see anyone, and believe me, I've replayed my return visit to the shack time and time again in my mind. If he didn't see me, obviously he wouldn't know who I am. Maybe he heard me walk up the path or drive up. The thing I'm worried about, and Jeff, I haven't even mentioned this to you, is that if he did see me, and if he finds out who I am, he may think I saw him and want to murder me to get rid of a potential witness. Does that make sense?"

"Unfortunately, it does," Jeff said, "but I sincerely wish it didn't. I've been thinking the same thing, but I didn't want to alarm you. You really need to be careful until the killer is caught. Promise me you won't take any chances. Will you do that?"

"Yes, I promise."

Laura spoke. "Jeff, have you talked to the sheriff today? Has he found out anything? On the outside chance that the killer finds out who Marty is, it seems to me we need to find the murderer and find him or her fast."

"I spoke with the sheriff on the way here. He told me the BLM was able to get a court order to remove the artifacts and put them in storage before returning them to the tribes. He said they have no leads or clues at this time."

"I assume Marty's name is in the official report as the one who discovered the body."

"Yes," Jeff said, "but that's not a public record. The only people who have access to that information would be someone associated with the sheriff's department. If you're asking if the killer could get that information, the answer is no."

"I have a thought," Laura continued. "Since there was no fingerprint match on the cigarette butts, and I know this is a long shot, but I remember you telling us last night, kind of as an aside, that you spent a lot of time yesterday with Lucy at the Hi-Lo. You said something about her having the strange ability to remember license plate numbers and what brand of cigarettes someone bought."

"Laura, I think I know where you're going," Marty said. "If we could find out who bought that brand of cigarettes, and if the person had a car with a license plate Lucy remembered, we might be able to find out who was smoking the cigarettes. It's a real long shot because we don't know if the killer bought some Desert Springs cigarettes at the Hi-Lo, but maybe, just maybe, he or she did. It wouldn't mean he or she was the killer, but it would give us more information." She looked across the table at Jeff.

"If I get a license plate number from Lucy, can you run it for me and tell me who the car is registered to?"

"Easily, but what do you intend to do with that information? Remember, you promised me you wouldn't take any chances."

"Jeff, I have no idea what I'll do with the information. A few things would have to fall into place. Lucy would have to remember both who bought the cigarettes and the license plate number, and then you'd have to run it. It would be premature for me to try and answer your question, but I'll tell you one thing, I'll be at the Hi-Lo when it opens in the morning."

"You'll get the information you need from her, and she'll tell you about someone you need to talk to," Laura said.

"How do you know?" Marty asked.

"Trust me. Some things I know. This is one of them."

CHAPTER TWENTY-THREE

True to her word, Marty was at the Hi-Lo the following morning when it opened at eight a.m. She walked in and saw Lucy sitting in front of her computer. She imagined Lucy was checking to see what photos needed to be developed that day.

"Morning, Lucy. Checking to see what photographs came in after the store closed last night?"

Lucy looked up abashedly. "Nah. 'Member I tol' ya' 'bout how I have a thought of the day, kinda tryin' to make me a better person. Well, jes' checkin' different sites to see what works fer me today."

"Well, did you find one?"

"Yeah. It's a quote by some guy named John Wooden. Never heard of him, but here's the quote, 'Do not let what you cannot do interfere with what you can do.' I think it means nothin's impossible. Whaddya think?"

"I think that's exactly what it means. I believe he was a famous basketball coach at UCLA years ago. He had a very positive approach to coaching and was always saying things like that to the members of his team. They probably took it to mean they could score every time or make every free throw or something like that."

"Think my problem is I was always tol' by my dad I couldn't do things 'cuz I was a girl. Who knows, maybe if I'd had a dad like John Wooden I'd be a nuclear engineer or something'."

Thinking of Lucy as a nuclear engineer definitely tested Marty's imagination, but she replied, "Could be, Lucy, could be. I've got a couple of questions for you. Jeff said you and he were talking the other day, and you mentioned you always remembered who bought what brand of cigarettes and you also remembered license plate numbers." She took a baggy out of her purse and carefully withdrew the Kleenex covered cigarettes.

"Do you remember selling this brand to anyone?" Marty asked, holding her breath as Lucy looked at the cigarette butts.

"Only made one sale of 'em in the last week. Think I tol' ya' 'bout the guy. Didn't look like he belonged here with his fancy haircut and clothes. He's the only one who's bought any Desert Springs cigarettes in I dunno how long. He's the one who wanted to know where Randy lived. Why ya' askin'?"

"I'll get to that in a minute. Since he didn't look like he was from around here, he probably drove here from Los Angeles or some other big city. Any chance you remember what he was driving?" Marty's heart was pounding so hard in her chest, she was sure Lucy could hear it.

"Have to be a blind man to miss that shiny black Caddy Escalade he was drivin'. Must be some rich guy to have a car like that one. I 'member it cuz we don't get many cars like that drivin' thru High Desert. Know they got a lot of 'em in the Springs, but we're out of the way up here in High Desert. Ya' probably want his license number, too."

"Do you remember it?"

"Course. Like I tol' yer' boyfriend Jeff, it's one of them things I can't help. I'll write it down fer ya." She handed Marty a piece of paper with the license number on it and then looked at Marty shrewdly. This have somethin' to do with Randy's murder? Ya' tryin' to solve it? Hear ya' was the one who found him."

"Lucy, I don't know, but it very well might. If it does, you'll be one of the first to know. Thanks."

"Wait a minute. Don't think ya' ever met my cousin, Mary BirdSong. Her side of the family stayed with the Agua Caliente tribe, and my side didn't meet the tribe's requirement for membership. Anyway, Mary and I been like sisters. We're the same age, and we see each other a lot. Matter of fact, that's why Randy started comin' in here, because of Mary. Saw her last night, and she ain't takin' his murder well. Says she thinks she caused it. Wouldn't tell me nothin' more 'bout why she said it. Might wanna talk to her. She's grievin' purty bad."

"I'd very much like to talk to her. May I say you suggested I get in touch with her?"

"Course. Here's her phone number. She lives on the reservation down in the Springs, but she lived with Randy fer a lotta years, so she might know somethin'. Gotta tell ya' it was lonesome at the Road Runner last night. Missed seein' him sittin' at the bar with his bourbon and branch water. He was always there. Didn't seem right fer him not to be in his usual place. Uh-oh, boss is givin' me the stink eye. Think I better get to work. Call me if ya' find out somethin."

"I will, Lucy. Thank you so much."

She hurried to her car and called Jeff. "Jeff, I have a license plate number for a man who bought some Desert Springs cigarettes from Lucy. He was the only one who's bought any for a week. He must have been out at Randy's because he was the one who asked Lucy where Randy lived. I think we're getting closer to finding the killer." She read off the license plate number to him and said, "I'll call you later. I have another call coming in on my phone."

She punched a button and said, "This is Marty Morgan."

"Ms. Morgan, Rich Willis gave me your number. I'm the one he referred to as the undercover agent for the BLM. Before we begin to have a conversation, I'd like you to know I'll be recording it, and I'd like your assurance that anything we say will be strictly confidential between us. Can you promise me that?"

"Yes," she said in a curious tone of voice.

CHAPTER TWENTY-FOUR

"I've never talked to an undercover agent before, so I have no idea how this is supposed to go," Marty said.

"I'll help. First of all I won't be giving you my real name. That might jeopardize my cover. What I am going to tell you is I had scheduled a meeting with Randy Jones the afternoon you discovered his body. I've been working with him for over five years. In order to gain his confidence, I've had to sell him some Native American artifacts that were obtained illegally."

"You must be Colin Sanders."

"That's the name I go by. The only reason I'm telling you this is because at some point in this investigation you probably would have tried to get in touch with me, even giving my name to the sheriff and perhaps other law enforcement personnel. When you never heard anything back from them about me, your suspicions may have been aroused, and you might have tried to go to the media, and then I would really have some problems. Does this make sense to you?" he asked.

"When you put it that way, yes. I assume you were given the photographs I took of the items at Randy's place."

"Yes, and I thank you very much for them. They're a huge help to us. I was supposed to meet with Randy the afternoon he was murdered on the pretext I was interested in buying his collection. He had telephoned me about it. As soon as Rich heard Randy had been murdered, he called me and told me not to go out there that afternoon. I'd planned to examine the pieces and then the FBI was going to take over and arrest Randy for possessing them and offering to sell them, both of which are crimes."

"It must have really thrown your plans into an uproar when Randy was murdered."

"You have no idea. I suppose the good news is the BLM has gotten a court order to move the artifacts to a safe place, so they can be given back to their rightful owners. The other good news is that with my reputation as a dealer in black market Native American artifacts, more people are coming to me to buy things, which means exposure to even more people who might have other black market items that hopefully we can repatriate over a period of time. It just takes years."

"I'm rather surprised you're telling me all this. Aren't you afraid I'll blow your cover?"

"No. I understand you're in a relationship with Detective Jeff Combs, and he's known to be one of the most honest and ethical law enforcement officers around. From what I know about him, there's no way he'd get into a relationship with someone who didn't meet his high standards. Secondly, of course we investigated you. There is absolutely nothing in your past or present to indicate you'd be a threat to us. From what we found out, you're a very discreet appraiser, and we decided that would carry over into this area. And lastly, the reason how you came to discover Randy's body speaks volumes. An appraiser who would turn down an appraisal from which she could make thousands of dollars because of ethical concerns is someone we felt we could trust."

"Thank you, and you definitely can trust me. I just wish the killer could be caught. Quite frankly I'm a little freaked out thinking he may have seen me, and at some point in time he might identify me and be afraid I know something. I left some papers with Randy when I was there that had my name, address, and phone number on them. I'm hoping he didn't get them, and that they're safely in the possession of the sheriff or Rich. I have to tell you I'm not sleeping very well because of my concern about this situation."

There was a long pause. "I'm not surprised to hear that, and I'm sorry. Marty, I don't quite know how to tell you this, but the sheriff and Rich told me they thought it was strange that you hadn't left any information about your appraisal with Randy."

"I did. I left my estimate of how much the appraisal would cost and the length of time I estimated it would take me to complete it. If the papers weren't there, that means the person who killed Randy must have taken them, and it also means the killer knows who I am."

"I'll call Rich and Luis and tell them that you did leave paperwork with Randy that had your name and contact information on it, and there is a very good possibility that the person who killed Randy has it. They definitely should know about this. I probably don't need to tell you since you're around Detective Combs a lot, but I'm sure he's already told you to be extra careful. If you see or hear anything you think is suspicious, please call one of them. I'd also like you to promise me that you'll tell Detective Combs about this development. The murder wasn't committed in his jurisdiction, but I'm certain this is information he'd want to know."

"I will, but I have to tell you I have goose bumps all over my body. I feel like going home, locking my door, and staying in bed until this is over." She touched her eyelid and tried to make it stop twitching. It didn't.

"That doesn't surprise me," the man she knew as Colin Sanders said. "To change the subject. I had copies made of the photos you took at Randy's, and they really are a huge help to us. If it ever should come up why we were investigating Randy, one look at those photos will convince anyone that we had reason to. An heir or someone intent on making trouble for us could always claim we brought in stolen pieces to make it look worse for him than it was. They could say we tried to set him up. Your photos show otherwise."

"Thank you. I assume we'll never meet, but I'm glad I could play a part in returning to the tribes what never should have been taken from them in the first place. What you're doing sounds terribly dangerous, but I have to say I'm glad you're doing it."

"I'm sure a lot of people would think that having a government official sell something that is illegal to a collector is a serious waste of tax dollars, but I think of it as a sting. Just like you hear about stings involving drug raids, well I work with stings involving Native American artifacts. I have to go now, but I wanted to personally thank you for what you did. Like you said, we'll probably never meet, but I've enjoyed talking to you."

"Be careful, and thank you for your service. What you're doing for the Native Americans is long overdue."

Well, I can scratch Colin Sanders off the list of suspects. I think I'll see if I can get ahold of that doctor when I get home. Wonder how long it will be before Jeff has a name to match up with that license plate number I gave him. Plus, I need to call Lucy's cousin, Mary BirdSong, and see what she knows. If she lived with Randy for a long time, I might be able to get some information from her. Looks like I'm going to have a busy day. I just hope no one other than Duke is waiting for me when I get home.

CHAPTER TWENTY-FIVE

When Marty parked in front of the compound she was halfway expecting to see someone lurking near the gate or next to the side of the house, but the only thing she saw was Duke in his customary spot waiting for her. John and Laura were gone for the day, and Les was working in his art studio. She could hear music coming from it when she got out of her car.

"Duke, I wasn't gone that long, so you should be fine. I need to make a phone call. Come on, let's go inside."

She sat down at her desk and retrieved the doctor's business card from the desk drawer she'd put it in when she'd come home late yesterday afternoon. A cell phone number had been written on the back, and she thought she'd probably have a better chance of reaching him by calling that number. Receptionists who worked in doctors' offices often felt they had an obligation to protect their bosses, and one way of doing it was by waiting until the end of the day to give them their messages.

Punching numbers into her phone, she sat back and hoped he'd pick it up rather than having to listen to a recorded message. In just a moment she heard, "This is Dr. Lowenthal. How may I help you?'

"Doctor, my name is Marty Morgan. I was talking to an antique dealer in Palm Springs, Carl Mitchell, and he told me you have a very fine collection of Native American artifacts. I was wondering if I could have a few minutes of your time."

"I'm always interested in talking to people about that subject, but it will have to be short. I'm scheduled for surgery in a few minutes."

"This won't take long. I'm an appraiser who was preparing to do an appraisal for Randy Jones. I was led to believe that you know him, in fact, Randy told me he had scheduled a meeting with you about possibly buying his collection."

On the way home from the Hi-Lo she'd been thinking about how she could approach the subject of Randy, and she'd finally decided to just be honest. She wanted to see how he reacted. She knew it was a risk, but if he was the killer, he already had her personal contact information, and if he wasn't it didn't matter.

"I met Randy several times at Native American artifacts shows. We talked a few times, and he said he had some very good pieces. I told him if he was ever interested in selling them, to call me. He did call me, and we set up a meeting for the afternoon I understand he was murdered. I've thought about it a lot and wondered if I had made it to the meeting if I would have been murdered too. You see, I had to do an emergency follow-up operation on a patient of mine, John Seymour, who developed complications from a prior surgery I'd performed on him, and I wasn't able to keep my meeting with Randy. It happened so fast I never even had a chance to let Randy know I had to cancel the meeting. I was planning on calling him the next day, but then I read in the paper that he'd been murdered."

"I see. Yes, you may have been very lucky. By the way, Doctor, what hospital are you associated with?"

"I do all of my surgeries at Desert Regional Center Hospital. Why?"

"A friend of mine in Los Angeles has been told she should have a knee replacement. I've been trying to get her to have it done here in the desert, so she could stay with me while she recuperates. Thanks."

"No problem, but I don't understand exactly why you called me."

"Doctor, other than the killer, I was the last person to see Randy Jones alive, and I feel I have an obligation to find out, if I can, who's responsible for killing him. The more people I can eliminate, the closer the authorities will be to finding the killer. You've just been eliminated."

"Well, I think this is a first for me. Don't believe I've ever been thought of as a murderer, although there have been times I thought I could kill for a certain artifact, but fortunately, I've never acted on it," he said laughing. "I have to go now. Good luck with your friend, and if she does decide to come to the desert for her surgery, please recommend me."

"That I promise," Marty said as she ended the call feeling a bit guilty about her white lie. She'd wanted to find out the name of the hospital, so she could double check that he had actually been in surgery on the afternoon of Randy's murder.

Ten minutes later the person she spoke to in the surgery center at the hospital confirmed that Dr. Lowenthal had indeed done a surgery on the afternoon in question. Marty wasn't very proud of herself for telling the person that her father, John Seymour, told her he'd developed complications and had to undergo a second surgery. She'd told the person her father had a history of lying to his out-of-state daughter to get her to come and see him. She said she'd been out of town on business and just picked up her messages. The woman Marty spoke with said she remembered it because it had been an emergency, and she had to reschedule several other surgeries in order to accommodate Dr. Lowenthal. She still wasn't very happy she had to work past her quitting time in order to do it.

That's two down, Marty thought. *Time to see if Jeff's found out anything.*

When she called Jeff he said, "I was just getting ready to call you."

"Does that mean you were able to find out the name of the man who owns the Cadillac Escalade?"

"Not only found out his name, I also found out a lot about him, but from what you've told me about Randy, they are quite an unlikely pair."

"Lucy said the same thing. I'm all ears."

CHAPTER TWENTY-SIX

"Jeff, I can't stand the suspense. Tell me everything," Marty said after finding out that Jeff had successfully located the owner of the black Escalade through the license plate number Lucy had remembered and given to her.

"I matched him instantly once I put him in the system. After I got his name, which is Luke Peterson, I googled him. He's been very successful in the video gaming field, so it was pretty easy to find out about him. A number of magazines have done articles on him. He's kind of a wunderkind, you know, one of those people who does incredible things at an early age." He spent the next few minutes telling her the story of Luke Peterson.

When he finished, she said, "I guess I could call the gaming company and ask to speak with him."

"I figured you'd want to get in touch with him, although I want to caution you that he could be the killer. Then what?"

"I don't know. Maybe I've got a little of Laura in me, but I don't have a bad feeling about him."

"If you're only talking to him on the phone, I don't think that's particularly dangerous. It might be a good idea to use your maiden name. Don't give him your phone number or your address. Can you promise me that?"

"Yes. That sounds reasonable. So do you think I should call the gaming company where he works?"

"No, through the miracle of modern technology and by calling in a few favors, I was able to get his cell phone number for you as well as his email address. I think that should work," Jeff said in a self-satisfied voice.

"Jeff, you're amazing. That is absolutely wonderful. I'm going to call him right now. I'll get back to you after I talk to him."

"Good luck and remember, be careful."

*****

A man's voice answered her call and said, "This is Luke Peterson."

"Mr. Peterson, my name is Marty James. If you have a few minutes I'd like to talk to you."

"I only have a few minutes before I have to attend a meeting. What can I do for you?"

She took a deep breath and began speaking, "Do you own a black Cadillac Escalade, and do you smoke Desert Springs cigarettes?"

He was quiet and then asked, "Why do you want to know? Those are very strange questions to just call up and ask me."

"Yes, I'm sure they do seem strange. I was told by someone you were asking for information about a man named Randy Jones. I don't know if you're aware of it, but he was murdered a few days ago. Several Desert Springs cigarette butts were found not far from where his body was discovered. I believe you were present at the scene of the murder. I'm helping the sheriff try to locate his murderer, and I'm wondering what you were doing there, when you were there, and if you saw anything that seemed to be strange."

She heard what sounded like sobs coming from the other end of the line.

"Mr. Peterson, are you all right?"

He took a deep breath and said in a ragged voice, "I recently found out that Randy Jones was my father. I've been trying to locate him for years. A private investigator I hired was able to find him through a photograph. It's a long story, but after he told me I drove to High Desert to find him. I wanted to talk to him, maybe get to know him. Since he'd never contacted me I wasn't sure what the reception would be. When I got to High Desert I sort of lost my confidence, and I turned around and came home. Two days later I drove up to High Desert again, intent on introducing myself. You can understand that, can't you?"

"Of course, and I'm so sorry. I was with him shortly before he was murdered, and he mentioned he had a son, but he didn't know where he was."

"My mother left him when I was two years old and took me with her. I won't bore you with the details, but I was subsequently adopted by a family and my legal last name became Peterson. Even if he'd tried to find me, he probably wouldn't have been able to because of my new adopted last name."

"Well, I guess that's something we'll never know."

"Let me tell you what happened. I went out to his place and parked quite a ways from where his truck was parked. I walked up the path and saw an old man sitting at a table in the shack with his back to the open door. For some reason I couldn't just walk up and say something like 'Hi, Dad, remember me?' He looked old, so I was afraid if I did, it could give him a heart attack. I stepped behind a nearby large boulder and watched him from there. I was nervous, and I smoked several cigarettes while I was watching him, so those are probably the cigarette butts that were discovered. I never thought to pick them up."

"What happened next?" Marty asked.

"I saw a man approaching the shack and doing what I had done, keeping out of my father's sight in case he turned around. He had a tomahawk in his hand. I was pretty much in shock between seeing my father and then seeing some man with a tomahawk in his hand..." His voice broke, and he stopped speaking.

"Mr. Peterson, I am so sorry. The last few days must have been horrible for you."

He coughed and said, "You have no idea. I've relived the scene so many times. Anyway, the man quickly walked through the door, and then struck my father in the head with a tremendous blow of the tomahawk. He fell to the floor, obviously dead. Just at that moment, before I could react or scream out, I heard a car on the road below. The killer must have heard it too, because he ran out the door and disappeared. I was in complete shock having just watched someone being viciously killed. It was doubly worse for me because that someone was the father I hadn't seen for nearly forty years. I was panicked and didn't know what to do next. After waiting a few minutes to make sure the killer was gone, I made a bad decision. I ran too. I never saw the killer or his car when I drove away."

"Mr. Peterson, why didn't you contact the sheriff or someone?"

"I was afraid I'd be arrested for his murder. You know, the disgruntled and abandoned son finds his father and kills him. Who's going to believe the story of an accused killer? I didn't think there was any way someone would find me. How did you do it?"

She told him about Lucy and said she had some contacts in local law enforcement that had helped her. She also told him she was an appraiser and had been with his father just before he'd been killed, and that she was the one who had discovered his body.

"Do you think you could identify the man who killed your father?"

"Without a doubt. I've thought of going to the police, and see if I could get one of their artists to do a sketch based on what I would tell them, but I'm sure they'd want to know why I was at his shack in the first place."

"They probably would. I have a friend who's in law enforcement. Let me talk to him, and I'll get back to you. Again, I am so sorry for your loss. I hope you have people you can talk to."

"I have a very good therapist who I'm seeing daily. He's helping me."

"Good. You've been through so much, I'm glad you're getting some help. No one should have to go through something like that alone. I'll be in touch when I know anything."

"Marty, I'm glad you called. It feels so good to get this off my chest. I suppose this is one of those catch twenty-two situations. On one hand I found my father, but on the other hand, now he's dead. I really do need to get to my meeting. If you find out anything, please let me know."

CHAPTER TWENTY-SEVEN

"This is Mary BirdSong," the voice on the telephone said.

"Mary, my name is Marty Morgan. I'm a friend of your cousin Lucy's. She suggested that I call you. Let me tell you a little about myself." She told Lucy about the appraisal and how she came to discover Randy's body. "Lucy told me that although you and Randy were no longer living together, you still cared deeply for him. I was wondering if I could come and talk to you."

"I heard that some woman found Randy. I'm glad it was a business thing and not some woman he was involved with. I don't think I could have taken something like that."

"I don't know anything about any other women. As a matter of fact, I haven't heard anything that even leads me to believe he was involved with anyone else. I feel I have an obligation to see if I can help find the killer, since I was the last one to see him alive, other than the murderer. I need to go into Palm Springs this afternoon and was wondering if you'd have time to see me then. I'm starting an appraisal tomorrow and I'll be tied up for several days. I really would like to talk to you as soon as possible."

"I don't think there's much I can tell you. I haven't seen Randy since he told me he didn't want me to live with him anymore, but yes, I could see you this afternoon. Here's my address."

That afternoon Marty drove into Palm Springs and easily found Mary's address. She lived in a doublewide trailer on the reservation. Bright flowers had been planted in pots in front of her home, and an old green Buick was in the driveway. Clearly Mary cared about where she lived. In contrast to her neighbors, her lawn was neatly maintained, and her car looked like it had just been washed.

Marty walked up to the small porch and rang the doorbell. It was immediately opened by a rather unattractive middle-aged Indian woman wearing jeans and a t-shirt bearing the words, Agua Caliente Tribal Member.

"Hi, you must be Mary BirdSong. Thanks for seeing me this afternoon."

"Yes, I am, and you must be Marty Morgan," she said extending her hand to shake Marty's. "Please, come in. It's not very fancy, but I don't need much. I live here by myself, and it's plenty of room for me. I made some tea. Would you like a cup?"

"That would be lovely, thanks."

"I'll be back in a minute. Please have a seat and make yourself comfortable."

Marty sat down in a large easy chair and looked around the homey little room. Photographs filled every inch of the walls. Tribal photographs, photos that looked like family members, and even photos of early Palm Springs were displayed. As an appraiser of things that were generally from earlier times, Marty was fascinated by them. She stood up, looking at each one, contemplating how they illustrated a different time and a different way of living.

Mary walked in with their tea. "It looks like you're enjoying my photographs."

"Very much so. I would think the museum here in Palm Springs would be very interested in these, maybe even having a special exhibit for them. They provide quite a unique look into a very different way of life, both tribally, and for the City of Palm Springs."

"I keep telling myself I should do that, but I really don't want to part with them yet. Please sit down. What would you like me to tell you about Randy?"

"I don't honestly know. This is going to sound very strange to you, but I have a sister who is a psychic."

She was interrupted by Mary, who said, "Right. We get a lot of them out here in the desert. There's a group of so-called psychics out in the hills. They say they're fortune tellers and they read cards and tea leaves and all that junk. I've never known where it's ever helped anybody."

"Generally, I agree with you, but I will tell you that my sister was part of a paranormal study conducted by UCLA and at the end of the study they concluded that she had a very high level of unexplained psychic abilities. I've personally witnessed her ability to foresee things. Anyway, whether you believe it or not isn't important. What is important is that she told me I should talk to you about Randy's death."

"Did she say why?"

"No, just that you might be the key. Let me set your mind at ease. She said nothing to indicate you were involved in any way with the murder, just that you knew something."

Mary's eyes filled with tears and they began to flow down her cheeks. "Randy was a good man in many ways. He was good to me. Actually he was the only man who was ever interested in me. It broke my heart when he told me he didn't want me to live with him any longer."

"Do you have any idea why?"

She blew her nose and said, "I think he sensed I knew what he had in the cave. You told me you went in there, so it's no secret a lot of the things in there were illegal to possess, buy, or sell. I think because I'm an Indian he was afraid that I'd tell someone about them. And I did, but not when I was living with Randy." She looked down at her crossed hands and started sobbing. "I think I'm the one responsible for his death."

"What do you mean?"

It took Mary several minutes to become composed enough to talk. "I told Richard Sagebrush about the things Randy had in the cave, and I'm afraid he killed Randy."

"Who is Richard Sagebrush? I've never heard of him."

"He and I grew up together on the reservation and have done a lot of things together to help our tribe. The older he got, the more concerned he was about the Native American artifacts that were being illegally taken from government lands and from sacred tribal grounds, even burial grounds. He's become a real fanatic about the subject. He regards it kind of like a holy war, and I wouldn't be surprised if he killed Randy so legal authorities would become involved, see what Randy had, and then give the stolen artifacts back to the tribes. I know it's twisted thinking, but I think he's gone way past the rational state. And it's all my fault. I know if I hadn't told him about the cave and all the things Randy had in it, he'd still be alive." She uncrossed her hands and lowered her head to her hands as if her body could no longer support it, so deep was her grief.

"I don't know what to do, Mary. I doubt if this Richard that you referred to will talk to me or the authorities." Marty suddenly remembered her recent conversation with Luke, Randy's son, and how he was certain he could identify the killer.

"Mary, I have an idea. You have so many photographs here. Do you have one of Richard Sagebrush?"

Mary's tears had subsided, and she stood up. "Yes, we were honored by the tribe last year for the work we've done for the young people of the tribe, particularly with the bird songs. That's where I got my name. My father was one of the most famous bird singers around." She walked over to the wall across from where she'd been sitting and lifted a photograph off of it.

"Here. Richard is the one standing next to me. We're the only two people in the photograph. May I ask why you want it?"

"I spoke with a man who happened to be on Randy's property when he was murdered. I'm not at liberty to tell you who he is or why he was there. He told me he had a very clear view of the man who murdered Randy. He actually saw the murder take place. May I take this photo with me? I'll give it back to you in a couple of days. I'd like to show it to this man and see if Richard is the man he saw on the day Randy was murdered."

"Yes. Whoever murdered Randy did a terrible thing, and if it's Richard, he should be punished. As much as I'd hate to find out that one of our own tribal members killed Randy, his punishment would certainly send a strong message to our youth that no matter how high your status is in the tribe or anywhere else, you must obey the law."

"Thanks, Mary. I'll let you know what happens. And please, don't blame yourself. Remember, Randy was the one who knowingly broke the law. You didn't have anything to do with it. As soon as he bought his first illegal artifact, events were set in motion which had nothing to do with you."

"I feel better after telling you about Richard. It's all I've thought about since I found out Randy had been murdered. Please call me and let me know what you find out."

"I will," Marty said and then she walked out to her car, opened the trunk, and carefully put the framed photograph in it.

CHAPTER TWENTY-EIGHT

Marty's meeting with Mary had lasted longer than she'd planned, and with the other errands she had to run in Palm Springs, it was dark when she drove back to the compound. As she approached it she noticed a car that appeared to be abandoned off to the side of the road and made a mental note to tell Jeff about it. She saw a bumper sticker on the back bumper with words on it that read "Tribal Power."

She parked in front of the compound and saw Duke waiting patiently for her at the gate. She walked into the courtyard and waved to Laura, Max, John, and Les. "Hey, Marty, we were wondering where you were. Jeff called and said all he got when he called you was your voicemail. He said to tell you he was running a little late. Since you weren't here, and I got off early, I walked Duke a couple of hours ago, but he's probably ready for another walk," Laura said.

"Well, that's good, because I'm running late, too. I need to get on the computer, and then I'll walk Duke. See you in a few minutes. Come on, Duke." They walked into her house, and Duke immediately walked over to his dog bed and fell sleep.

Marty changed into dark jeans and a navy blue blouse. She walked outside to the rear of her car and carefully removed the photograph of Richard Sagebrush and Mary from the trunk. While she was doing it, she thought she heard the sound of a car nearby, but she didn't see any headlights, so she decided it must have been her imagination.

Good, she thought, *the photograph's small enough I can scan it on my computer and send it to Luke.*

Marty spent the next few minutes scanning the photograph and composing an email to Luke asking him if he recognized the man in the photograph whose name was Richard Sagebrush. She wrote that she had reason to believe he might be the murderer. She asked him to let her know one way or the other if he recognized the man. She went on to say that if he did recognize the man in the photo he should notify Detective Jeff Combs of the Palm Springs Police Department by email. She ended the message by giving Luke Jeff's email address. Jeff would know what to do with the information if Luke recognized him. She wasn't sure the sheriff would take the information from her. She attached the scanned photograph and pressed send. It was on its way.

"Okay, Duke. Time for me to put your booties on and take you for a walk. Might as well do it now before Jeff gets here, and John serves dinner. John's not happy when his dinners are interrupted."

She and Duke walked towards the gate that led outside of the compound. Marty turned back to the group who was enjoying a glass of wine in the early spring evening. The weather was perfect in the desert this time of year. "I'm taking Duke for a walk. Be back in a few minutes. If Jeff comes before I get back, tell him I'll only be a few minutes."

They walked through the gate, and it swung closed behind them. The night was jet black, and the only things visible were the stars overhead. Marty never put Duke on a leash when they did their nightly walk, because it wasn't necessary. The compound was on two acres of desert land, and there was no one around.

"Duke, let's go behind the compound. We haven't been there for a while and since it's too dark for me to clean up anything you might do, no one will inadvertently step in something they'd rather not have on their shoes." They walked along the compound fence, Duke several steps ahead of Marty.

When Marty was about twenty yards from the compound she felt something cold pressed into the middle of her back. She put her hand behind her, intending to brush it away when a male voice said, "We're going to take a little desert walk. When I kill you with the gun you just felt, no one will hear it because there's a silencer on it. May be a few days before anyone discovers you out here. It's a pretty remote place."

Marty kept walking and the only thing she could think to do was buy time by talking. Maybe it would keep her alive long enough for a miracle to happen. "Who are you, and why are you doing this? I have a boyfriend who's a cop, and he'll be here in a few minutes."

The man didn't answer her. She glanced over her shoulder and even as dark as it was, she recognized the man behind her from the scan she'd just sent to Luke. It was Richard Sagebrush. The pieces of the puzzle suddenly tumbled together in her head.

"You're Richard Sagebrush, and you're the one who murdered Randy Jones. You did it so the artifacts would be repatriated to their rightful owners."

"Yeah, and you're next. It really was sheer genius on my part to find a way to get those things back to where they belong, and I didn't have to wait around for years for it to happen. I'm not sure, but was I worried you may have seen me at the scene of the murder. I got your name and address from the papers I grabbed off the table at the shack. Once you're gone, no one will ever know it was me, and everything will be returned to the rightful owners, just like they should be. I know there will be more I'll have to repatriate, but this one is over."

The night was so dark she didn't think Richard saw Duke off to the side curiously looking at the man with Marty. She thought maybe Duke knew at some level that something was wrong, because his tail wasn't wagging. She knew she was no match for the man who was behind her holding a gun against her back. She yelled, "Duke, go home! Now!" Her only hope was that when Duke got to the compound alone, someone would realize that Marty wasn't with him, and something must be very wrong, because he was never far from her.

"That's enough talk. No one can help you now. Keep walking and start saying your prayers. Your time on earth has been reduced to minutes. Saw you walk out with that dog and knew he was no threat. A German shepherd, a pit bull, or a boxer might cause me some grief, but a Labrador retriever wearing pink booties? Don't think so. It's so dark out here I'm having a hard time seeing things, but I remember from when I was walking this property earlier today that there are a bunch of palm trees and cactus bushes in this direction," he said, motioning with his hand out to the side. "We'll go behind them. Think it would be a good idea if you knelt when we get there. Something kind of fitting about a person being murdered when they're on their knees. When their body's found, it will be obvious they were begging for mercy.

"It's kind of like what the Indian women and children did at Wounded Knee, but the soldiers killed them anyway. Sort of ironic you're in the same position only the tables are turned. Now it's an Indian killing a white woman," he said.

I should have told Jeff how much I care about him. I should have told Laura she's the best sister anyone could ever have, even if we do argue, and she makes fun of my twitching eyelid. I should have…

"This is the place. Get on your knees, and put your hands together like you're praying. That'll look good when they find you if there's anything to find once the desert animals are finished with you."

Marty lowered herself to her knees and prayed for a miracle.

CHAPTER TWENTY-NINE

Jeff turned off the computer in his office, said goodbye to the captain, and walked out to his car in the early darkness. He was tired and looking forward to another good meal at the compound and seeing Marty. It was getting to the point that he was beginning to dread the days he didn't see her.

I don't know whose court the ball is in, Marty's or mine. I think she cares for me as much as I care for her, but it's pretty obvious she's not going to invite me to live with her in the compound. I think the only way that's going to happen is if we're married, and I'm not sure I'm a good marriage risk. Maybe I'm too old to start all over again. Plus, there's a very good chance she'd say no even if I did ask her to marry me.

He spent the thirty minute drive to the compound going back and forth about whether or not he was ready to get married, always acknowledging that even if he asked her, Marty might say no.

As he approached the compound he noticed a car parked alongside the road. He drove past it and saw a bumper sticker on it that read "Tribal Power." *That's a strange place for someone to leave their car*, he thought, *plus with that sticker, it looks like it's someone from one of the tribes. Must have run out of gas. If it's not gone when I leave the compound later tonight, I'll call it in.* A few moments later he parked in his usual place in front of the compound. The computer in his car started flashing with a new message. He read it and gasped. The message was from

Luke Peterson regarding the scanned photograph Marty had sent him earlier.

He looked at the computer screen and saw what Luke had written. "The man in the photograph who you identified as Richard Sagebrush is definitely the man I saw at the shack when he killed my father. I understand that Detective Combs will give this information to the appropriate law enforcement officials. Let me know what you want me to do. I'll be happy to come to High Desert and identify him in a lineup or give a statement. I'll wait to hear from you."

Jeff ran to the compound gate and was opening it just as Duke came running up to him. He had his pink booties on, but Marty wasn't with him. He hurried into the courtyard and shouted, "Where's Marty?"

"She took Duke out for a walk about fifteen minutes ago. Why?" Laura asked.

Jeff pulled his gun from its holster and said to Duke. "Find Marty, Duke, find Marty." Duke raced towards the gate with Jeff right behind him. He yelled over his shoulder, "Stay where you are. Don't try to follow me. Marty's in trouble."

"I'm going with you. She's my sister," Laura said.

"No. Les, make sure she stays here." He ran into the dark night, trying to follow Duke who blended into the night. Several minutes later Duke stopped and stood next to him. He could hear Marty softly crying and begging the man he now knew was Richard Sagebrush to spare her life. He made a vow at that moment that if he was able to save Marty's life he was going to ask her to marry him. He slowly crept to within a few feet of where Richard was standing over Marty. He got close enough so that he could make out Richard's silhouette and could see the gun he was holding that was pointed at Marty's head.

Jeff's years of training and instinct took over and there was no thought process involved. He simply raised his gun and shot Richard, hitting him in the arm that was holding the gun and causing him to drop the gun. He had the brief thought that the years he's spent at the gun range had paid off.

"Move and you're a dead man, Sagebrush. Marty, it's okay. You're going to be fine. Duke and I are here. I know you're really shaky, but I want you to pick up Sagebrush's gun and walk over to me.

"Good. Put the gun at my feet. Here's my cell phone. I want you to call Sheriff Antonio and tell him to come to the compound and arrest Richard Sagebrush for Randy Jones' murder and your attempted murder. After you call him, call Laura and tell her to bring Led and John and a flashlight to the back of the compound. I'll yell when I see them, so they know where we are. And lastly, you better call Duke over to you. He's quivering and shaking like crazy, and I'm sure he needs to know you're all right. Duke was the one responsible for me getting here in time, so we both owe him a debt of gratitude. I can feel you shaking. Here, go ahead and lean against me. The others will be here in a few minutes, and very soon this whole incident will just be a memory."

CHAPTER THIRTY

Several hours later, John said, "Well, I'm glad I hadn't started dinner when all this happened. What a night. Is anyone still hungry?"

"John, we're always hungry for your food, but I think having a couple of glasses of wine has been good for all of us. Jeff, what's going to happen now?" Les asked.

"Sagebrush will be arraigned more than likely tomorrow morning. I'm sure he'll hire a good attorney. From what I hear the members of his tribe have received a lot of money from the casino they own, so he can probably afford it. Anyway, I'm sure his attorney will tell him to plead not guilty, and then the judge will set a trial date. His attorney will try and get him out on bail, but being charged with murder and attempted murder is pretty much a guarantee that the judge won't allow him to get out. Then there will probably be a plea bargain offer. If he agrees to whatever it is, he goes to prison. If he doesn't agree to it, he stands trial and will go to prison, probably for life. No jury in their right mind would acquit him."

Marty walked out of her house with Duke next to her and joined them at the communal table in the courtyard. "I just got off the phone with Mary BirdSong and Luke Peterson and told them what happened. I feel so sorry for both of them. Mary feels everything is her fault because she was the one who told Richard about Randy's artifacts. It's going to take her a long time to get over it, if she ever does. And poor Luke. He finally found his father, but never even got to talk to him. It all seems like such a waste. Truth really is stranger than fiction. No one could ever make up a story like the weird facts in this case."

"It's kind of funny that I told Max to stay home and relax tonight, and it's the one night we have a lot of excitement out here. He's never going to forgive me for that," John said.

Marty shuddered. "Trust me, that's the kind of excitement I never want to go through again. I really thought I was going to die when I bent down on my knees in the desert. Duke, Jeff, you saved my life."

"Sometimes you get lucky and get to where you need to be before something horrible happens. It was kind of one of those things, but I agree, I don't want to ever go through something like that again. I honestly didn't know if I was going to be able to get to you in time," Jeff said, gently placing his hand over hers.

"Okay, I think we need to eat something. Tonight it's bratwurst with coleslaw and baked beans. I know that doesn't sound too gourmet, but it's leftovers from The Pony. Don't despair. I do have a surprise for dessert, but I could use a little help. Les, Laura, why don't you two do the honors on the barbecue for the brats. I've been simmering them in beer for hours, and they should be really plump by now. Slap them on the barbecue for eight minutes or so to finish them. Marty and Jeff, stay where you are. You've done enough tonight."

A few minutes later the courtyard became quiet. Jeff and Marty heard voices coming from the kitchen and by the barbecue outside John's back door, but with only the two of them remaining at the picnic table it was peaceful. Duke was snoring softly where he slept next to Marty.

Marty and Jeff both spoke at the same time. "Marty, I…" "Jeff, I…"

"You go first," Jeff said.

"All right. When I was being marched out into the desert by Richard, and I knew I was probably going to die, I realized I'd never told you how much you've come to mean to me. I love you. If you don't feel the same way, I think we better end this relationship because I can't be your friend." She took a deep breath. "Actually, I decided to ask you if you'd like to move into my place here at the compound."

Jeff stared at her in amazement. "Well, I made a decision tonight, too. I decided to ask you to marry me. I know I'm just an old detective, who's losing his hair and carrying a few too many pounds, but I love you, and while a few hours ago I would have been happy to move into your home, now I want to move in when we're married. Marty Morgan, I didn't have time to get a ring, but will you marry me?"

Marty noticed he was rubbing his finger and his thumb together, and she remembered Laura had mentioned once that it was a "tell," something he did when he was nervous. She felt her eyelid begin to twitch and laughed as she shouted, "Yes, yes, yes!"

At that moment Laura, John, and Les walked into the courtyard with several platters filled with bratwurst on buns, baked beans, and coleslaw. "What's the yes, yes, yes, I just heard?" Laura asked

Marty turned to look at her, "Laura, would you be my maid of honor? Jeff and I are getting married."

The platter of bratwurst sandwiches Laura was holding dropped out of her hands and landed on the courtyard paving stones with a crash. Laura looked first at Marty and then at Jeff. "Are you kidding me?"

"Nope, this is for real. We're going to get married, and then Jeff is moving in here."

"All right," John said, clapping his hands. "You can have the wedding here, and I'll make all the food for it as my wedding present. Laura, I think we can salvage the sandwiches. I'm invoking the five second rule," John said, bending down and giving Marty a kiss on the cheek.

"What's that?" Les asked.

John answered, "In restaurant talk if someone spills something on the floor they have five seconds to get it back on the plate. Supposedly it's okay to eat it if it hasn't been on the ground any longer than that. Think Julia Child popularized it on her television food show. Since we're not in a restaurant, that drop actually might qualify as a ten second drop. Fortunately I have a killer dessert for you, if we can't eat the sandwiches."

"I'll bite, literally," Laura said. "What's the killer dessert?"

"It's a dessert a little old Italian grandmother gave me the recipe for called Zucotto. It's kind of a chocolate pudding. Trust me on this one. No matter what your day has been like, you can't eat just one serving."

An hour later, the other four fully agreed with John that no one could eat just one serving.

RECIPES

GAZPACHO

Ingredients

1 ½ red bell peppers, cored, seeded, and chopped into ½ inch pieces
1 large cucumber, peeled, seeded, and roughly chopped
½ red onion, roughly chopped
½ cup water
2 stalks celery, roughly chopped
14 oz. can of crushed or chopped tomatoes
1 ½ fresh ripe tomatoes, cored, and roughly chopped
1 garlic clove, crushed
½ cup ready-made salsa
¼ tsp. cayenne pepper
1 tbsp. lemon juice
1 tbsp. dried Italian herbs
1 tsp. garlic salt
2 tsp. Worcestershire sauce
½ tsp. red pepper flakes
3 tbsp. red wine vinegar
1 tbsp. olive oil
1 tsp. Kosher salt
½ tsp. fresh ground pepper
2 tbsp. fresh cilantro, roughly chopped (for garnish)
1 ripe avocado, chopped into small square pieces (for garnish)

Directions

Place the chopped bell pepper, cucumber, celery, onion, half of the canned tomatoes, and the water in a blender. Pulse until the chopped vegetables have been further chopped to a consistency you like. Add the remaining canned tomatoes, fresh chopped tomatoes, garlic, vinegar, red pepper flakes, olive oil and Worcestershire sauce, and blend.

Add the salsa, cayenne pepper, lemon juice, Italian herbs, garlic salt, Kosher salt, pepper and blend. Chill for at least 2 hours. When ready to serve use chilled soup bowls and spoons (30 minutes in the freezer) and garnish with a drizzle of olive oil, a little chopped avocado, and a sprinkling of cilantro.

I like my gazpacho to have texture, but I dislike large chunks of anything in it. Serves 4 to 6. Enjoy!

SEAFOOD PAELLA

Ingredients

3 tbsp. extra-virgin olive oil
2 sweet Italian sausages, casings removed
1 skinless boneless chicken breast cut into ¾ inch cubes
¾ tsp Kosher salt, plus extra for seasoning
¾ tsp. freshly ground black pepper, plus extra for seasoning
8 large cloves garlic, peeled, and thinly sliced
1 medium leek, white and light green parts only
1 medium red bell pepper, stemmed, seeded, and diced
3 8 oz. bottles clam juice
15 oz. can diced tomatoes in juice
1 tsp. smoked paprika
¼ tsp. ground turmeric
1/8 tsp. cayenne pepper
3 bay leaves
8 oz. spaghetti, broken into 1" pieces

12 small little neck clams OR half a bag of frozen clam meat
12 large shrimp, peeled and deveined
1/3 cup roughly chopped fresh Italian parsley

Directions

Heat the oil over medium high heat in a large Dutch oven. Add the sausages and stir, breaking them into small pieces with a wooden spoon until cooked through, about 4 minutes. Add the chicken, ¼ tsp salt and pepper. Cook until the chicken is no longer pink on the outside, about 2 minutes. Transfer the chicken and sausages to a medium bowl, using a slotted spoon.

Add the garlic, leek, onion, bell pepper, and ½ teaspoons salt and pepper to the pan. Cook until almost tender, about 5 minutes. Add the clam juice, tomatoes with their juice, paprika, turmeric, cayenne, and bay leaves. Add the spaghetti and cook, uncovered, until almost tender. Add the clams and shrimp.

Cover and cook until the clams open, about 5 minutes. Discard any unopened clams. Remove the cover, reduce the heat to medium low, and simmer gently until shrimp and chicken are tender, 5 minutes. Remove the bay leaves and discard. Season with salt and pepper. Mix in the parsley and serve. Enjoy!

CARROT CAKE WITH CREAM CHEESE FROSTING

Ingredients
2 cups flour
2 tsp. baking powder
½ baking soda
1 ½ tsp. salt
½ tsp cinnamon
½ tsp. nutmeg
2 cups sugar
4 eggs
1 ½ cups almond oil

2 cups grated carrots
1 8 oz. can crushed pineapple, drained
1 cup chopped walnuts or almonds, optional

Directions

Preheat oven to 325 degrees. Grease and flour a 9" x 13" pan. Mix together first 7 ingredients. In a separate bowl beat the eggs until light and fluffy, then beat the oil into the eggs. Add egg and oil mixture to dry ingredients and beat well with an electric mixer. Add grated carrots and pineapple. Stir in nuts, if desired. Bake for 50-55 minutes. When cake is cool, frost with Cream Cheese Frosting.

CREAM CHEESE FROSTING

Ingredients

½ cup butter, softened to room temperature
8 oz. package of cream cheese, softened to room temperature
2 tbsp. orange juice
1 lbs. sifted powdered sugar

Directions

Combine butter, cream cheese, and orange juice, and beat together until creamy. Gradually add powdered sugar, beating well. If needed, add more powdered sugar to get desired consistency. Enjoy!

ZUCOTTO (FLORENTINE PUDDING)

Ingredients

½ cup shelled almonds, chopped
14 oz. sponge cake or lady fingers (you can buy these at the store)
½ cup of liqueur (brandy, orange) for non-alcoholic use coffee
1 ¾ pints of heavy cream, chilled

¼ cup sugar
1 cup chocolate (not less than 50% cocoa bean content) sliced in thin strands
For garnish you can use unsweetened cocoa powder, roasted almonds or hazelnuts and extra chocolate

Directions

Preheat oven to 350 degrees. Place the almonds in a fry pan over medium heat and cook until they're brown. Cool completely.

Lightly wet a 2 quart bowl and line with plastic wrap, allowing it to hang over the rim.

If using sponge cake, slice it thinly and cut each piece in half diagonally. Use about 2/3 of the pieces of cake or lady fingers and line the bowl, laying slices with the narrow ends pointing to the bottom of the bowl. Sprinkle the cake with liqueur and set aside. The moisture will allow the pieces to mold to the bowl.

Melt half of the chocolate and let it cool.

To make the filling whip the cream and the sugar together at a very low speed until it forms soft peaks.

Fold in the nuts and the remaining chocolate. Transfer 1/3 of the filling to a separate bowl and fold in the cooled chocolate.

Spoon the "white" cream mixture into the cake-lined bowl spreading it against the sides to create a well in the middle. Spoon the chocolate mixture into the well and level with a spatula. Lay the remaining cake slices/lady fingers on top and sprinkle with liqueur. Cover with plastic wrap and refrigerate for at least two hours.

To serve: turn the pudding upside down on a large plate. Remove the setting bowl and the wrap. Decorate as your wish. Enjoy!

PECAN CARAMEL CANDIES

Ingredients

63 miniature pretzels
1 package (13 oz.) Rolo candies
63 pecan halves

Directions

Preheat oven to 250 degrees. Line baking sheets with foil. Place pretzels on foil and top each pretzel with a candy. Bake for 4 minutes until candies are softened – they will retain their shape. Immediately place a pecan half on each candy and press down so the candy fills the pretzel. Cool for five minutes and refrigerate for 10 minutes or until set.

Amazing Ebooks & Paperbacks for FREE

Go to www.dianneharman.com/freepaperback.html and get your FREE copies of Dianne's books and Dianne's favorite recipes immediately by signing up for her newsletter.

Once you've signed up for her newsletter you're eligible to win autographed paperbacks. One lucky winner is picked every week. Hurry before the offer ends.

ABOUT THE AUTHOR

Dianne lives in Huntington Beach, California with her husband Tom, a former California State Senator, and her boxer puppy, Kelly. Her passions are cooking and dogs, so whenever she has a little free time, you can find her in the kitchen or in the back yard throwing a ball for Kelly. She is a frequent contributor to the Huffington Post.

Her other award winning books include:

Cedar Bay Cozy Mystery Series
Kelly's Koffee Shop, Murder at Jade Cove, White Cloud Retreat, Marriage and Murder, Murder in the Pearl District, Murder in Calico Gold, Murder at the Cooking School

Liz Lucas Cozy Mystery Series
Murder in Cottage #6, Murder & Brandy Boy, The Death Card, Murder at The Bed & Breakfast

High Desert Cozy Mystery Series
Murder & The Monkey Band, Murder & The Secret Cave

Coyote Series
Blue Coyote Motel, Coyote in Provence, Cornered Coyote

Website: www.dianneharman.com
Blog: www.dianneharman.com/blog
Email: dianne@dianneharman.com

Newsletter
If you would like to be notified of her latest releases please go to www.dianneharman.com and sign up for her newsletter.